THOMAS BRANIGAN MEMORIAL LIBRARY
Las Cruces, New Mexico

RUSTY IRONS

Books by Dan Cushman

Fiction
c. 1

RUSTY IRONS

by Dan Cushman

WALKER AND COMPANY
NEW YORK

All the characters and events portrayed in this story
are fictitious.

First published in the United States of America
in 1984 by the Walker Publishing Company, Inc.

Published simultaneously in Canada by John Wiley & Sons
Canada, Limited, Rexdale, Ontario.

ISBN: 0-8027-4031-6

Library of Congress Catalog Card Number: 83-40412

Printed in the United States of America

10 9 8 7 6 5 4 3 2 1

Chapter One

So stately his form, and so lovely her face
That never a hall such a galliard did grace.
                                        —*Marmion*

Rusty was home again, which didn't make Ma too happy. She said he was more trouble than he was worth. Also, he'd been seeing Grace McKibbin again even though the General had warned him to stay away.

"You awake?" whispers Rusty.

"Huh?"

"Be quiet. Bring your duds outside."

He had come in through the kitchen. He never slept in the house. He had his own place in the harness room. I got up barefoot on the cold floor, quiet as a person could be, but *squeak!* went Ma's bed.

"Henry, is that you?"

What could I say?

"What are you doing up? What time is it?"

How would I know, dark as it was? I didn't even own a dollar watch.

"I couldn't sleep on account of the sorrel mare."

"You're talkin' wild. Why, she ain't near due."

"Anyhow, I want to have a look."

"If you have a foreboding, take the gun."

"I got the six shooter."

5

"Take the rifle!"

She had no faith in a pistol. She couldn't hit the broad side of an ox with one and thought nobody else could.

"Everything is all right. Go back to sleep."

There were still some stars, and mist hung over Wildhorse Springs. The springs were famous, and it was why our ranch was where it was. Pa was a real old-timer and had had his choice. At that time you could smell mint, and the tobacco smoke that always hung on Rusty. I could foller him in the dark. I never got the habit, myself.

What he wanted was for me to ride for strays and stay at the old Post cabin. At least that's what he *said* he wanted.

"I got to tell Ma."

"No, she'll ask a lot of questions."

I had some questions, too, but I knew better than ask. Rusty would never tell you a thing until he was ready.

However, I was stubborn, too, and he finally gave in and said, "Go ahead. Tell her we're going to be gone about two days."

It really worried her when I went anywhere with Rusty. She said he picked evil companions. It worried her when I went off alone, too. She'd had terrible premonitions ever since Pa's body had been found, but that had been two years come August, plenty of time to plug me if they'd had a mind to.

Rusty was at the lower corral with Old Brindle, my favorite long horse. He had chosen Flyer, a big dapple bearing a Flying A brand. Both saddled! It was truly an *event* when Rusty saddled somebody else's horse for him!

"What's afoot?"

"Why, us Irons boys are going to attend the meeting!"

"What meeting is this?"

"The Association meeting."

The regular Roundup Association meeting was not until June.

"Whereabouts?"

"McKibbin's," he said without a tremor.

Brig. General Otis H. McKibbin, Ret., owned the Long M which was, second to ours, the oldest brand on all the high prairie between the Musselshell and the Missouri River badlands. It was actually McKibbin & Giehl, but Giehl was a pork packer from St. Louis who seldom troubled himself.

"How come Ma ain't going?"

"Because she don't know about it."

I wouldn't want my readers to think we were pulling out and leaving Ma alone. We had Dad Marsh, our cook, and three cowboys, not including Ardis Cribb, who broke horses on shares.

"The Association drumming us out, or something?"

No answer. Rusty would tell me when he was good and ready. He never let me forget I was just a slick nut kid. He was third from the oldest in our family, which was the Irons family, whilst I come along last. I was the "straw that broke the camel's back," Pa used to say. Ma had had twelve, five dying in infancy. It was a hard climate, so those who survived were good and tough, which was just what the country needed, that's what Pa said. He said Ma had done pretty well, everything considered. She grieved for the lost ones, however. She would hear them whimpering in the night and get up to look. She would walk around the

7

yard in her bare feet and Pa would have to go out and coax her back.

"There's nobody there. I'll bring the lantern and prove it."

"But I heard Baby Ella just as plain!"

This child had died at about one year and was buried at Beartown, away over in the Rockies.

"Why, Thelma," Pa said, "that little child is at rest in the arms of Jesus."

"Yes, of that we have divine assurance, but I *heard* her."

I have two sisters living, Pauline and Nelda, both married, in Nebraska and Missouri; a brother Clint on the police force in Reese River, Nevada; and another brother, Walter, last heard of in South America. Cecil fell before a hail of bullets during the Sweetwater trouble, and Pa had been shot by unknown assailants. Hence Rusty, Ma and yours truly made up the Irons clan insofar as the home range was concerned.

On the whole we are a family of large physique. I take after Ma's side being solid and square-faced. "Shut your mouth, Henry, the flies will crawl in!" she used to tell me. Nobody ever said that to Rusty. He favors the Ironses, who are tall and hip-sprung. A lot of swagger and *ya-hoo*, and that sort of thing, but well liked. Fellows would do anything to be accepted as Rusty's friend. And how the women took to him! (Therein lies the tale!)

Our big social event was the schoolhouse dance. Everybody went, young and old, and the babies would be put to bed in the wagons. There'd always be some woman there who was married, and would, as Pa said, "get her tail out of the crupper," and wouldn't you know it? She'd take out after Rusty.

"I'll not go to another dance while he disports himself that way," Ma would say. "I'll not sit there while he shames us."

Or maybe he'd bring some woman who was "fast." One time over at Fort Steele he and Bob Gooding really came a corker! They squired two women of about twenty-four, all powdered and perfumed and dressed to the nines, introducing them as the daughters of R.T. Miller, wealthy Three Forks banker, just back from the East. They were nothing of the kind. They had picked them up out of a bawdy house in Bozeman City and driven them all the way in a hired rig. There was a great to-do about them. Leading citizens like Tom Glynn and Benj. Rimmel were taken in completely, as were their wives; but the principals in this charade were not content with mere victory; no, they got to cavorting and carrying on wilder and wilder, and some of the talk got pretty raw and close to the bone, let me tell you! Finally Monte Sallows, who was floor manager came around and said, "Boys, you have had your fun, so now get these women out of here," so they did. Oh! was Ma waiting for Rusty when he got home! It was a week later, and she'd been saving it:

"Bringing those fallen women was an insult to every decent person in the hall."

"It was only a joke."

"If that's your idea of a joke it tells something about *you!*"

They got to going it pretty heavy, and as usual she brought up the name of Maude Herring, who was a married woman, but as she has nothing to do with this story I won't get into it. Rusty said it was a healthy thing for married women to frisk around once in a while and see what the other men smelled like, it was what a dance was for, and Ma said if he really believed that he was *depraved*. She couldn't understand it because they had always given him a Christian home, etc., until finally he slammed out of the house.

"You'll get shot!" Ma yelled after him. "One of these days you'll cavort with the wrong fellow's wife and that will be the end of *you!*"

He stayed clear of both Ma and the house most of the time, and if he was home you would likely find him lying on his bed in the old harness room, looking at the ceiling. He ate there, too. Dad Walsh would carry a special plate to him. Dad had to stop at the door and rap. Not even bosom friends such as Preacher Harlow or Lucius Engate, "The Ringbone Kid," were so bold as to walk right in. It was his castle.

Rusty had stopped chasing Maude and all other such women about one year before. He had reformed, but it had nothing to do with Ma's lace-curtain lectures. It came about because of Grace McKibbin, Brig. General McKibbin's only daughter . . .

The Brigadier was a widower twice, with three children. He had one son, Otis, Jr., who was a lawyer back East; another son, Stanhope, was supposed to manage the ranch, but he spent most of his time in Helena, our territorial capital. Stanhope could have been a doctor, and had studied in several colleges, but all he did was sit around in hotels, or if home he read, loafed or fished. He was a pointed foot in a square boot, Ma used to say. Then there was Grace, their half-sister.

She was much younger and still in school. The Brigadier had her enrolled in Roanoke Academy, Dexter, Ohio. I'll never forget the first time I saw her. It was the summer previous when she got in on the stage at Fort Steele. She had quality, and was so fine. She just seemed to float down. She couldn't help being sweaty and dusty, that long stage trip, and her dress was wrinkled behind so you could see the shape of her, but it didn't make any difference, because she had a real deep-down quality. I'd have been afraid to touch her, I felt so awkward and dirty; not that I was tempted. "Oh, thank you so much!" she says to the freight handler who got down her trunk, and give him the sweetest smile; it showed how nice she was. Then her father, the Brigadier, came out of the bank, and just stood there, on the steps, looking at her. You could see she was the *apple of his eye.* Then he tossed his cigar aside about half smoked and walked across—a very precise and gingerly walk—grabbed her, and lifted her right off the ground.

"Oh, Papa!" she cried, "don't do that!" Then she cast both arms around him and gave him about three big hugs. And they walked away together, and his carriage came, and she gave the coachman a big hug and kiss, too. He was a colored man, Sgt. Carrow, a retired Army orderly, all dressed up in parade livery for the occasion.

The scene now shifts to Musselshell City. This was a river port, about forty miles to the northeast. The big Missouri River boats came in there. It had just had the biggest river season in its history, also a railroad had been mapped through to Canada with a bridge at that point, hence optimism reigned, and they staged a Fourth of July celebration second to none. Everybody went. Fort Steele was all but deserted. Soldiers came from as far away as Fort Keogh (Miles City) to drill and play the parade tattoo. There were two bands, races, an oration by A.M. Chamberlain, baseball, songs and recitations, fireworks, etc., and a bowery dance at night. This latter was outside, under the stars, on a specially laid floor, with willows nailed all around, and Chinese lanterns.

I didn't dance, of course, never having learned how, but I was there watching and listening to the music. It was Prof. Giddings' three-piece orchestra from Fort Steele. Ed Walgate was the caller. It had just nicely started, about two square dances along, when Grace McKibbin arrived. She was with Millie Chamberlain, the two Nelson girls, and several young gentlemen— Paul Genser, Vincent Shields, Bill Lukens and young Dr. Giles. They made up an eight for the square dance, and traded off one and another for the fancy figures, or round dances, such as the waltz, schottische, varisonne, etc.

I hadn't seen Rusty till a very spirited scottische started up and there he was dancing with Grace McKibbin! He just sashayed over and asked her, and away they went. It was only a rough floor, to be torn up next day, but that didn't make the slightest difference—they positively glided, they sailed! It was a big crowd, but in and out they went, never bumping and never missing a step.

Rusty had been to Sioux City and come home with a blue serge suit, a four-in-hand tie wide as your hand, and he wore gentleman's riding shoes, not boots; and she had on some kind of voile, or dotted Swiss, which made her seem to *float*. She held up her dress with one hand, and touched Rusty's hand with the other, and her little slippered toe would go out and back, and they would dip and slide, him partly lifting her. The music was wonderful—violin, cornet, and piano, with Prof. Giddings just more than coming down with the bow, giving it all he had. They finished and people simply went wild! They clapped and cheered so they had to play it over again. The music had been good all the while, but it seemed like Rusty and Grace had provided the dash and whirl that got things really off the ground.

However, it was spoiled for me because something drew my eyes over and there stood General McKibbin, straight as a rod, dead-faced, and *he wasn't smiling.* He was watching them with the coldest eyes ever seen in the head of man!

At midnight there was a plate lunch, but Rusty didn't try to horn in on the Chamberlains, Nelsons, etc., and if Grace ate with anyone in particular it was young Dr. Giles who had hung up his shingle just that year. They left before Home Sweet Home was played, when every man danced with the girl of his choice, and vice versa, so that never came up, but it must have been that she and Rusty had an understanding because a week later he rode all the way to the dance at Flatwillow School, fifty miles, and there she was, having come with the Tomlinsons.

The scene now shifts to our house. Ma: "No, she didn't just *happen* to go over there with Jesse and Madge Tomlinson! That is another one of your prevarications!"

"My *what?*" says Rusty, trying to make a joke of it.

"Prevarications! Lies, falsehoods."

She'd never been beyond third form in country school, but Pa had bought a set of Sir Walter Scott, twelve volumes, from *Waverly* all the way through *Fair Maid of Perth,* and she'd read them to us out loud. Rob Roy was my favorite.

"The McKibbins don't go around with the Tomlinsons," she said. "Ten-cow ranchers are rubbish beneath the McKibbins' feet."

"Grace isn't that way! She was just visiting Marge—"

"No, she wasn't *just visiting.* She set out for that

dance, alone, on horseback. And she was riding *astraddle.* It had been *arranged.*"

"Riding *astraddle?*" Rusty cried, laughing.

"Yes, astraddle!"

"She was wearing a perfectly decent riding skirt. Where do you get all your information, anyhow?"

"You arranged that meeting. Let me tell you something! You're not up against Sid Herring now. You're dealing with the Brigadier! You'll find out he's not the one to stand by whilst his minor daughter chases with a man like you."

"Like *me?*"

"Yes, like you! You're a seducer and a fornicator! Such is your common repute. Why, she's a fifteen-year-old girl! You're eleven years older."

"Oh, the hell with this!" and out he rushed, got his blaze-face gelding Maccabee and rode off, spurring.

It was certainly unusual to see him in that sort of a state, because as a rule he responded to trouble as cool as ice. All you'd ever see was maybe a tightness about the eyes. He might hum a little tune under his breath. And always careful with a horse. Later he could be seen lying on his bed in the old harness room.

"Come on in, Hank."

He was lying with boots on in the iron bed, hat tilted over his eyes. Papers and magazines were strewn about. He was a great reader, especially of Bill Nye, and could reel off his stuff by heart. Around about were souvenirs of his many travels: a bone salmon spear, his obsidian collection from Yellowstone, ruby silver in white quartz worth $35, a silk corset which was a trophy of the Baroness Vichette, famed faro dealer and courtesan; and guns—pistols, shotguns, rifles. The place always smelled of horse because he never walked anyplace, just rode. I mentioned that he had his boots on; he had on his spurs, too, and the metal of the bed was all dug shiny from the rowels.

"You don't think I'd do anything to lose this ranch, do you?"

"Nope. What brought that up?"

"Ma. She's worried about the General."

As a matter of fact he brought in just about all the cash we saw with his estray business, and was the main rock standing against the big outfits with their Eastern backing that bid fair to take over the whole Wildhorse range.

"We're just as good as they are, kid."

"Sure are!" says I.

"Anyhow, the McKibbins have always made me welcome. Stanhope took me to dinner at suppertime when I was in Helena. And as for the Brigadier, he's cold toward everybody."

This was on a Wednesday. On Friday he set off to pay Grace a visit. He didn't say he was, but you could see that something special was up because he had Ardis clean his saddle and brush down Midnight, his favored horse of the moment, until his coat just simply *shone*; and he shaved, and clipped his moustache, and put on his new Panama hat. On his way he must have stopped and picked a bouquet of flowers. It was time for sweet flags along Goose Creek. I was told he arrived with a bunch in a wet handkerchief. Also a white shirt, which he freshly donned.

Thus arrayed Rusty arrived and was about to open the gate to the ranch yard, but the Brigadier must have known he was coming.

"Irons!" stepping forth with a rifle. "Stop where you are!"

Naturally, he did.

"You're not welcome in this home!"

"I was invited."

"I'm sure you are mistaken. I'll not have you attending my daughter."

Rusty asked why.

"Because you have a reputation such that no decent man would have you associate with his family."

It was just as if he'd been talking to Ma!

There were several reports on this, and one had the Brigadier call him a "scamp and a womanizer," which didn't sound right to me. I mean you couldn't imagine him using those words. What he did say was this, and it galled Ma worse than anything—

"Let me give you a word of warning. Don't attempt to revenge yourself. I know well enough the code of you shanty folk. If you defy me in this or lift a hand I'll have you and your tribe hunted down and scourged from the land like cur dogs."

. "Where does that imitation general get off calling us shanty folk?" Ma yelled. "Why, the Ironses was one of the best families in Kentucky. They were people to be reckoned with, let me tell you! They were there early as 1800 and owned slaves and fine horses. They were quality at a time when the McKibbins were still in Ireland, eating potatoes. His father came here during the famine. They were pig-in-the-parlor Irish and worked in the collieries. The very Negro slaves in Ironses' service lived better than the Irish. The Ironses would have ridden them down with their steel hoofs."

Then Ma lit in on Grace, saying she was nothing but a young mare allowed to run with the bit in her teeth. "She chases men and they get the blame for it. She goes around unchaperoned riding astraddle. She shows her leg to anybody that'll look at it."

I had to say *something*, so I said she seemed all

right to me, and Ma said, "Well, you got a lot to learn about how decent and respectable girls should act. She's giddy, chasing after men too old for her, unchaperoned at dances!"

Later Ma relented some, saying the poor little thing might not be to blame entirely. What could one expect, having such a father? He had fancy women in Helena reached by his own private stairs, through doors opened by his own key, and they were "perfumed parlors of dalliance and lust," a term she had got from the sermons in the *National Revivalist*. And she said there were even worse tales about his son who was "not entirely normal," which she wouldn't go into because I wasn't old enough.

"Go do your chores. You'll be sullied by this world soon enough."

This was about the last of July. The *Fort Steele Tribune* came along saying Miss Grace McKibbin was sojourning in the capital, and the *Helena Herald*— Pa had subscribed to papers from near and far and after he crossed over the Great Divide they kept coming unpaid and unbidden—arrived in due course to say she was amongst the guests at a rose and voile picnic in Mountaindale Park, and next that she had departed for school in the East together with "Misses Vernlaw, Ackerman and Chamberlain."'The train must have got her there in a hurry because hardly a week later I picked up a letter from her addressed to "Russell Irons, esq." postmarked Manfred, Ohio; no return of any kind, but I knew it had to be hers—the absolutely beautiful penmanship, and the perfume which filled our mail box (tight oak to close out mice, pack rats, etc.).

Didn't show it to Ma; left it on Rusty's bed where he

found it when he got in a couple of days later. "Thanks," he says, and there was a new bond between us.

The letter was the first of many, and I never pried into the contents of a single one. Not so Ma, I'm afraid. It was roundup time and I was away from home, earning a side fee of 25 cents per head serving as rep for the Swaller Tail outfit, so she was the one who got the mail. When I got home there were two letters laid out and you could smell not only the perfume but the scorch coming from being held close to a lamp chimney to read what was inside. If Rusty noticed he made no remark. He would get a letter and you'd see him with the lamp burning away late as he composed an answer.

It came winter and the letters stopped. Rusty departed and not one arrived thereafter. I wondered if they'd met someplace. It turned out he was in Diamond City running the Square Deal Stable while Sid Foster was attending the legislature, so her letters went there. He came home in the bleak spring. I mentioned previously that he was in the estray business. How this worked was as follows: cattle would be passed over in the roundups; he would gather them and advertise for auction. Critters that got off their "customary range" (a legal term), could be held for reward. Badlanders, homesteaders and "free cowboys" would drive them in and Rusty would pay from $2 up. He would advertise all stock in the Fort Steele paper, and he had a tailcoat lawyer named Vost Funderhide, so all was according to Hoyle. You see, it was illegal to *rebrand* cattle. You could a horse, but if you rebranded your own cow you broke the law. This was to make it tough on rustlers. If they stole your cow and shipped it the inspectors in South St. Paul would send payment to the owner of record as shown in the brand book. People were always getting money for some critter they thought was still on the range which had been shipped by accident. Or, say there was some stray bull they wanted to get rid of, they'd just load it on the cars and it would be ground into bologna when the cheque arrived. As a result Rusty had trouble getting paid unless he went back personally, in the caboose, so he often drove to Castle, the silver town, where the butchers asked few questions; and this time he announced he was going to drive all the way to Deadwood, Dakota Territory, where the famed gold mines were cut off by the warlike Sioux!

On this daring exploit he took his bosom friends, Preacher Harlow and the Ringbone Kid; also a rowdy character named Jack Evans; Tom McCall, our erstwhile deputy sheriff, suspended for unspecified reasons; an Indian guide by the name of Bird Watch, who spoke the Sioux tongue; and a number of others who wanted free transport to the land of gold. They got through without a hitch. Their chief trouble was not Indians but the dearth of grass and water. They sold for $10 per hundredweight, live, and came back with gold sponge in a weight of 88½ ounces, troy, the lion's share going to Rusty as a matter of course.

Then, still during the school year, Grace came home. By prearrangement, it was natural to assume. Not so. She came home by herself, unexpected, and Rusty didn't even know. He was off in Castle. Her father was in Sacramento at a railroad meeting, and Stanhope was in Helena. She returned all by herself by stagecoach to Fort Steele and then out to the deserted ranch by livery. Just the winter crew was on hand, and the big house was in the charge of Mr. and Mrs. Skinner. Even the China cook was wintering in San Francisco.

"That girl has been expelled!" Ma said. "She can't go back East and carry on like she does here. They'll put up with just so much and no more. Those are strict schools for *decent* young ladies."

Ma was afraid she'd come over to our place looking for Rusty, and laid plans for dealing with her, but it didn't happen. She went back to town and stayed with the Nelsons—at least there was something in the paper about her winning the cakewalk award at a necktie-and-gingham social, "with her stalwart consort Dr. Giles"—and Ma breathed easier. The Brigadier came home, Stanhope came home, and Rusty rode in at our place. That was how things stood when he woke me and this tale opens.

Chapter Two

And darest thou, then, to beard the lion in his den,
the Douglas in his hall?

—Marmion

We rode most all day across the McKibbin domain, and came up on the bulge over Goose
Creek with a long view of the home ranch,
late sun shining on roofs, and the lines of rail fences.

"There she is!" says Rusty, proud enough so's
you'd think he owned it. You'd sure never guess he'd
been halted at gunpoint and told he was not welcome.
"Finest house in the territory. Put together like a piano. Every stick came in by steamboat."

"So I hear."

"Never been inside? You will tonight."

Actually I'd been there with Ma, but to the porch
only. We rode along the creek, losing the view, and
crossed about five bridges coming in through groves
of box-elders, still not in blossom. The main gate was
open, and somebody drove in ahead of us. I had a hard
time breathing, such was my apprehension, but
Rusty didn't seem to have a care in the world. He
hummed a little tune all the while.

"Look at that barn!" he says. "Built to U.S. Army
specifics!"

Tom Gregory of the Anchor brand was ahead of us

at the horse trough. A little step-and-a-half fellow hopped around taking care of his team. No heed paid us, but we were on horseback, which was a different thing. Up at the big house I could see Amos Hoffner of Enterprise Land & Cattle, and Lee Dougherty the Association attorney, amongst others. And stiff at his parade-ground attention watching us was the Brigadier!

I must have flinched, but not Rusty. "Rest your mind. We got every right to be here."

"How about the horses?"

"I'll show you what to do with them. And our gear, too. Better put it under cover. Plenty of room in the barn."

"We sleeping here?"

"Why not? Don't be bashful, little brother."

He had a long drink from the pipe. He drank and drank whilst his eyes roved, appraising the situation. Then it was my turn. It came from a spring some way off, cool but not cold. No match for our Wildhorse Springs water, but good. I took a long time, too, seeing how Rusty made out. They all greeted him with handshakes and good cheer. The Brigadier might have nodded to him, but in that I might be mistaken. Then a bright flutter and it was Grace! She sashayed out as if it was the most regular thing in the world, and took Rusty's hand in welcome. You'd have thought nothing had happened, and he had not been driven off at gunpoint, and they hadn't written, and she hadn't come back before end of term, or anything. But it lasted only about a dozen words, and she went flying back inside. It looked as if things would pass without trouble after all.

I wish I had a whole chapter to describe the McKib-

22

bins' barn. Immense is the one word I'd use, red brick sides with windows and a roof of many low pitches, a whole acre of shingles sloping to a gable and a square pigeon-cote ventilator with lightning rods and much iron decoration. The ventilator was topped by a weather vane in the form of a pacing horse in full stride. There were stalls in a double row, but no stock. The central passage was big enough to store carriages. At one side were some quarters used by Sgt. Carrow, the coachman. He came forth and saluted, a very fine, courteous darky, white wool on head and cheek, still imposing in physique though somewhat stove up.

"Good evenin', Mist' Irons," he said.

"Good evening, Mr. Carrow," I answered, because Ma always told me I had to call a colored man by as good as he called me, or otherwise I'd prove I wasn't so polite as he was.

"Can I hep' you with yo' horses?"

"I can manage. I'll turn them in the corral, but I need a stall for our gear."

He took me to a box stall at the far end, about a quarter up with hay. I moved our stuff in, and was still at it when Rusty came.

"Hungry?"

"Gosh, yes."

"We'd better dig down and find some clean shirts. We're going to eat at the house."

"At the table?"

"No, barbecue. The meeting will be inside."

I didn't have a clean shirt, but I stripped to the waist, washed, and put the old one back on. Rusty had a fresh white shirt with blue stripes, and a low, hard collar. Some of the people had white linen shirts, but on the whole I looked up to average. The barbecue was wheeled around in a cart, and some stood and ate, but others sat in on the porch at one of several tables. These were covered with the whitest linen you ever saw. The napkins were about two feet square. You could choose between mutton and pork, no beef. It was my first time with a barbecue that wasn't beef, except one time with buffalo. Besides meat and drippings there was potato, camp biscuits, hominy and lemon pie. Coffee. An Indian girl and a Chinaman went around with refills. After eating we each got a Havana cigar in foil.

"I'll put mine away for by and by," says I.

The women had a party of their own under an arbor. That's where Grace was, the hostess, paying to Rusty not the slightest heed, nor he to her. After a while, when it was almost dark, the lights were carried inside to a large room with chairs and benches. Everybody could sit where he liked. I drew a straight chair with a cane seat, and Rusty sat in a low slung rocker beside me.

"This meeting will come to order," says the Brigadier, rapping with his mallet, or gavel. "Mr. Dougherty?" and sat.

Lee Dougherty has already been mentioned. He was our Association lawyer and recording secretary. A tall, fine-looking man, Roman in bearing, with silvered hair in a feather-edge cut, he stood to get attention.

"We will dispense with the reading of the minutes of our last meeting because this is not a meeting *per se*. We deal with special matters." This was for our benefit, the Ironses having been left out. Not only were we not invited, they figured it was the one place Rusty wouldn't dare show up. However, there we were, and Dougherty smiled a bit ruefully. He then set out to say something about the public domain, mentioned this ruling from the Interior Department, and that by the Department of War, and about opening the Blackfeet and Assiniboine lands north of the river, "an area the size of Vermont, comprising no fewer than ten million acres," or some such figure. "We must make sure our precedence is honored in this region!" he says, spread-eagling to show how much they needed him to watch over their affairs. "We must insist that livestock of the contiguous proximity move naturally into this vast reach of virgin grass, so lately left fallow by the thundering bison. In this regard I have written our Territorial Representative."

He went on like this for about ten minutes, but finally he had built himself up as far as possible, so he turned to big, ugly-looking Amos Hoffner.

"I believe you have a presentment for this meeting."

"I do!" said Hoffner, getting to his feet. We were now going to find out why the meeting had been called without us!

He was very deliberate. He was built like a work stallion, thick through in every way. He had real heavy features—jaw, nose, and a ridge of bone over the eyes. His hair came down in a V, making him look stupid, which he wasn't, and obstinate, which he was. He looked like a bully, and might have been if the country would have stood for it. I'll admit to being afraid of him. He was head man with Enterprise Land & Cattle, a big corporation outfit from back East. They had bought up a number of old-time brands and gained control of the Willow Creek range. This was a strip about forty miles long south of the Wildhorse Hills. He tried to buy us, but Pa wouldn't sell. After he was shot he tried some more, but Ma had vowed to hold the place together. We never more than passing suspected him in Pa's death. It wasn't his style. But here's what he was capable of:

One of the outfits Enterprise had bought was the old Z Bar at Lance Coulee. This gave them the McGivneys for neighbors. There were seven of the McGivney boys, an untamed crew. They lived in a dugout cabin on the side of the coulee and ate out of tin cans, in general lived the life of wild animals. The law was always after them and half the time they didn't dare come to town for groceries, patronized the Indian traders instead. Enter Hoffner and Enterprise Land & Cattle. He sold off his old bulls and introduced Durhams, which bred the longhorns a heavier calf. Would have if the longhorn cows had had milk for them, which has later to do with the story. It brought him in conflict with the neighbors. Especially the McGivneys. They ran longhorns and paid no attention to where they grazed. The law of Customary Range meant nothing to them. They turned them loose and trusted the roundup to find them in the fall. Some of their steers would get to be six or eight years old. And some weren't *steers*, they were bulls. They would put their brand on a calf maybe not even throwing him down, and if he got away without being castrated they'd say what the hell! bulls won't stray as far as steers, they hang around the cows, etc. At any rate they had all these longhorn bulls which actually drove off the Durhams. Those short-horned eastern bulls just never stood a chance. Well, after about one warning Hoffner instructed his riders to shoot every stray bull caught on his range.

Andy, chief of the McGivneys, called Hoffner a lot of names, threatening to kill him if they met, and he spread the tale how Hoffner had killed a woman down in Wyoming. Hoffner had a lawsuit with a widow who was later found hung to a tree. The verdict was suicide, but Andy said Hoffner had paid a witness $400 to leave the country.

Shift the scene to Gray's Station on the old Army Road where they have a big horse auction. Everybody in the country was there including Andy McGivney and Amos Hoffner.

"I hear you been looking for me, Andy," says Hoffner, pleasant enough under the circumstances.

Oh, how Andy lit into him. He had a terrible, raucous voice and said Hoffner had knuckled to Eastern interests trying to run the pioneers off their ground, and attracted a quite a crowd. "You killed my bulls on the range!" yells Andy. Hoffner sprang and hit him in the mouth. He moved like a big puma. How he hit him! and down went Andy.

Andy lay there a second, and Hoffner would have let him get up, but Andy made the mistake of reaching for his gun. This I didn't see, but I saw the diving scatter of people, and BANG! Hoffner shot him. Andy had got partway up and it knocked him flat on his back and he lay there so awful still! I'd never seen a man shot before. It was my first experience, though by no means my last. The shocking thing was how he had just turned to nothing. He wasn't Andy any more. And the flies spun over him. The real tiny flies had smelled the blood and made a funnel. People said it always happened; they came from nowhere when a man was dead. Leastwise in summer.

Well, sickened I might be, but it didn't trouble

Hoffner. Not so you could notice it. No sir, he just rammed his pistol back in the scabbard; he carried it high up with the handle in because he used the cross draw; and he looked around as if to ask, *are there any more McGivneys?* He made himself available, I'll say that for him. Of course there were others from his own outfit at hand, their number including Tex Mullans, his top hand, or ramrod, from Nebraska. No action from the authorities: self-defense.

So much for longhorn bulls. He had more trouble by far with the shareholders because the original manager had paid far too much for livestock. His name was Bassout (pronounced Ba-*soot*) and he just bought up ranches from in at town and took whatever livestock inventory happened to be on the books. Then the shortage had to be charged off to rustlers, winterkill or Indians. Hoffner took over and had the shareholders put through an assessment on stock—not livestock, corporation stock. They all had to chase old money with new or lose everything. Did he retrench? No sir! He brought in more cattle, and more. It was the half-time work of one cowboy just to chase his cattle back off our Organ Pipes range, but Ma refused to accept a penny of his money because he might use it to prove collateral rights (all range being public domain and preemptive in origin, maintained through uninterrupted use).

Hoffner then turned his eye on the Buffalo Sinks. This was a big piece of range lying between Willow Creek and the badlands. It was dry as a bone—worse than dry because when there was water it consisted of poison sinks, alkali with yellow stuff. The Geologic Survey dug down in one of them and found a solid fifteen feet of old buffalo bone, green stuff and hair. Yet tantalizing to the eye. How the grass grew! It waved, it rippled in the wind! Antelope ran across it like wraiths, white tails lifted, speeding off forty miles in a day. A fellow named Walter Braudy homesteaded in Nine Mile Coulee nearby, sank a well eighty feet and struck a very good grade of water. Hoffner bought him out. A mining man from Last Chance laid out the entire geology, including the depth of the sandrock layer that held the water, and next thing Hoffner was around putting up posts which claimed the subsurface water by reason of "discovery wells," a very dubious piece of legality. Nobody stopped him, so he set up a camp and started to drill. He used a horse-whim rig with what was called an Empire bit which went around and around, and for the deeper reaches brought in a churn drill that worked by steam. People would see this engine across the plains and think the railroad was coming. The Indians rode for a hundred miles and pitched their tipis to look at it. He sank fourteen wells in all. What he hoped for was artesian water, the famed "flowing wells of Camberwell" which needed no pumps, but the best he could get was halfway up the pipe. Pumps were required, and this meant force pumps, and for power, windmills. These were of large size but failed the job. Oh, we had wind enough! Ours is one of the windiest places in the West. But variable. How those rods would go up and down, but the water would give out. The pumps had to run submersed and pretty soon would start to howl. The packing would burn and the cylinders get red hot. Then the water would rise and whoof! you could see the steam for miles. He had to put men at each well to cut the power and/or prime them from a barrel of water. He set cowboys to this task, but they weren't up to it. They would be all alone for days on end, get lonesome and go someplace, be off shooting at targets, and the pump would go wild in a wind-storm and burn up. Hoffner had a terrible temper and he'd threaten to shoot the first man who left his post, but never did.

He was successful in pumping for about 1500 cattle when the shareholders came on a visit and decided not to put in any more money. So that's how things stood for him as we sat in the big room at McKibbin's.

"We are in an age of change," says Hoffner, striking a posture. He had a speech all worked up, that was plain to see. "The longhorn has had his day, and the four-year-old steer has had his day. No longer can we drive the hungry herds from the Rio Grande to harvest the grass of the North," and like vein. "We weep for the past," etc. "This is the day of steam, the boat that walks on water, and the iron horse," etc. But then he looked at Rusty, slouched in his rocking chair, and says, "It had been my intent to formulate an agreement to be presented by the various owners to the Irons interests, but I'm happy to see you came."

"You mean—" Rusty started to answer, but was gaveled down by the Brigadier.

"Order! Does party wish to be recognized?"

Thump! thump! went my heart, fearing this was the blowup I'd expected, but Rusty was as cool as could be:

"Party was addressed by the speaker."

"Nevertheless we proceed on order. Does speaker yield?"

"Not on your life!" cried Hoffner with a big ha! ha! "I have a presentment, here." He unrolled a big paper, actually an old map with another map drawn in crayon on the back. He fastened this to the back of a chair, which was too low, so he lifted it to a table. "Now, this is a map of the Buffalo Sinks and nearby areas, Army survey of '73." Using a wand he pointed out the Big Sink, the Little Sink, Chase Coulee, our ranch, the Wildhorse Springs, Uncle Will's homestead, and told the elevation of each. "The springs lie at 2,900 feet on the dot, descending to 2,800 where the Will Irons homestead house stands. Cottonwood Creek, famed for mountain trout."

True. Stanhope McKibbin used to come over and fish for rainbow trout using English lures; Cottonwood Creek flowing from our springs was the only place trout could be caught save for back in the hills, or across the Missouri River on the Blackfoot side.

"Mr. Chairman!" says Rusty.

The Brigadier dipped his head.

"May I address the gentleman?"

"Without objection, proceed."

"That line looks like a ditch."

"So it does, and so it is."

"You mean to dig a ditch right through our house? I'm not sure Ma would like that."

It got a laugh because as soon as Rusty spoke up people got nervous, suspicious of his temper.

"Ha-ha! Well, I wouldn't wish to set Mrs. Irons against us. No, what you refer to is a contour line, the twenty-nine hundred foot line. The twenty-eight foot line is right here. The ditch runs here, diverging, which indicates a descent of five feet per mile, allowing for a water flow velocity of two feet per second. As you see it doesn't start at the springs. The Wildhorse Springs are inviolate. We're interested in securing—at a fair recompense—water from the creek at Will Irons' homestead. Normal flow as of July 15 is 144 inches, correct?''

"Am I to answer? I don't want to be out of order.''

"Proceed," says McKibbin.

"How'd you figure any such figure as 144 inches?''

"The Army engineers so measured it in '75 and again in '76.''

"Why, '76 was the year of the Custer massacre. I recall we all lit out for Benton on the steamboat. No wonder they came up with 144 inches. That's over a man's head. Tall man's, too.''

It was all persiflage. He knew very well that the inch in this case was the miners inch, the amount which will flow through a hole one inch square, and not an inch deep across the whole creek. In Montana all the statutes are dictated by the miners. Stockmen suck the hind tit insofar as Montana law is concerned, unlike in Wyoming where they ride high in the saddle. Pa got elected to the Legislature one term and quit in disgust. "Money makes the mare go," he said, "and there's more comes out of just one gulch than the entire cattle range every single year." So much for that.

"The Irons are a mighty tall family," says Hoffner, resolved to keep his sense of humor, "and if anybody could keep their heads out it'd be you. But seriously, what do you say the flow is? After all you own the first water right.''

So he acknowledged it. I was afraid he might try and claim it to be a public property, at least when the creek reached Uncle Will's, seeing he had left the country. Will had taken 160 acres under the Homestead Act for Union Veterans, and added to it by buying soldiers' scrip, claiming eighty inches in all. Water right is a very involved thing and can't be severed from the land, but I don't pretend to be an authority.

"We have second water right, too," said Rusty. "We have all the water rights."

"No, you have first and second. Baker Transportation filed on third water right."

To make a long story short, Hoffner wanted to set up a steam plant on Uncle Will's homestead to lift water to where it could be ditched into the sinks.

"The plant could be situated here. We would have a lift of fifty-five feet, base level. Maximum of sixty-five to gain proper head. We require about eleven thousand feet of pipe. Stave pipe can be made in Helena for 25 cents per foot. I would propose a corporation subscribed to by those benefiting. My thought is also to allow the Ironses to run 200 head at no cost, or to put aside sufficient treasury shares to accomplish that end."

It sounded hunky-dory to me, because as things stood we were getting exactly nothing from the Sinks, and the water at Will's was just running off to the river. However, Rusty felt otherwise.

"As I see it," says Rusty, "you don't intend to charge Irons livestock a single cent to drink Irons water."

The *way* he said it, so easy and pleasant, cut like a lash. I was scared for a second that Hoffner was going to come for him, but quick of mind Dougherty horned in.

"Mr. Chairman. If I may make a few comments—"

"No, I'll handle this!" said Hoffner.

Rap! Rap! the Brigadier's gavel. "Order. Mr. Dougherty?"

"I have a legal point to make."

"Proceed."

"In regards the assumption which seems implicit in Mr. Irons' remark: he has used the term 'our water.' This implies he regards it as property, as if held in fee simple. As a matter of fact steam-flow is never a property. It is as the term states, a right, a right to use," etc., droning things over, until Rusty finally says,

"All right, if you say so, Lee. I'm no lawyer, but you're not lifting our water any sixty-five feet by stave pipe or anything else. I like it just the way it is, flowing down through the badlands. However, we only have second rights. You'll have to get hold of the owner, Will Irons."

"You administer the lands in absentia, don't you?" says Hoffner.

"Not me."

"You pay his taxes."

We did and there was no denying it.

"Then you thereby acknowledge authority."

"Correct!" cried Dougherty.

Hoffner ignored him, waiting for Rusty.

"This I neither affirm nor deny. At any rate I'm only one member of the family. How do you feel about it?"

He was talking to me. Everybody was looking at *me.* I sure would liked to get out of there, but I gulped and steeled my voice against the rooster squail which is my failing and said, "Nor I!" strong and firm.

"That makes two against, so I'm afraid you'll have to plan on locating below the Ironses' property line."

They couldn't, and he knew it. Beyond Uncle Will's the Coulee plowed right into the badlands.

"Is that your final position?"

"Why, Amos, nothing is final. As soon as I get a chance I'll lay the whole thing before Mrs. Irons."

On and on went the meeting, but its spirit was gone.

Chapter Three

Beware then, O errant knight, lest thy lovers bower become thy gibbet tree.

—Ivanhoe

At last we emerged under the stars. Ah, to breathe! Rusty stopped to talk, but I'd heard all the talk I wanted for one night and headed down for a good, long drink at the trough.

"Thanks, T.S.," Rusty said. He was talking to T.S. Gregory of the Anchor, which was actually a fallen T brand, but looked like an anchor bent around the side of a cow. "I'll look into it," says Rusty. Gregory had lost some cattle and wanted Rusty to keep his eye out. It shows we weren't in all-around disrepute on account of his estray business. He talked for a time, then he saw me, and linked my arm, saying, "Well, little brother," leading me off. It wasn't like him to choose my company, but he did, and we went to the barn, and down the mid passage, where the lantern gave long shadows, and there were empty stalls on both sides.

"Here it is. Is this all right?"

"This is fine." I wanted to lie down and talk but not him. "I'm rode out. Go to sleep."

My head buzzed from the excitement for a time, then I fell into a deep slumber, I was absolutely dead from travel and strife, and of a sudden something woke me.

I didn't know what it was. I listened and listened, and there wasn't a sound. That whole, vast barn was just absolutely quiet, yet something had brought me awake.

"Rusty?"

No answer. I felt for where he slept. His blanket was tossed to one side. The hay under it was not even warm. Out in the runway, by distant lanternlight, I could see posts and braces, and shadows, and one of the shadows moved.

Then a smell came to me and I knew it was the Brigadier.

If somebody had asked me did I know his smell I'd have said no, absolutely not, but I did. I lay there hardly breathing, wondering what he was about; and finally he cleared his throat, and spoke,

"Irons?"

"Huh?" says I.

"You're the boy, aren't you? Where's your brother?"

"I don't know."

"Weren't you sleeping together?"

My mind darted around like a gopher in a box. "He was here but he went someplace. He likes to sleep out under the stars."

"Don't lie to me, boy!"

"I ain't. He does like to sleep under the stars."

Rusty's idea of a good place to sleep was the Windsor Hotel in Denver. He could rough it with the best, but only when necessary. However, the Brigadier left and I lay hearing every hoot owl and coyote in the land until in the gray of dawn Rusty came back. Quiet as a mouse so as not to wake me he lay down, and I could smell *him.* I could smell him, and Grace, too.

The same smell as in the mail box when her letters came, only stronger, and somehow very disturbing. Finally I spoke,

"McKibbin was here."

He jumped like I'd touched him with a branding iron.

"When was this?"

"Hours ago. I been lying awake."

"What did he say?"

"Not much. Asked where you were."

"And what did you tell him?"

"Nothing, I didn't know where you were. Said you liked to sleep out under the stars."

"Let's get away from here!"

"Fine with me!" And it was!

Found our horses, no difficulty. As usual at that early hour they were all atremble, and looked on you with a leery eye. Their hides trembled over their bodies when first touched. Patient yet on edge, and full of willingness as soon as they feel your weight on the stirrup. You have to be ready for them to jack-hop around some. We set off briskly into the rosy-fingered dawn. A couple of dogs were up, the Brigadier's curly retrievers, and took note without barking. The little step-and-a-half fellow who was a sort of yard flunky might have been watching. Later, from a distance, the first smoke from the cook house. We were free and clear and able to *breathe.* How good everything smelled, all the plants waking to greet the day, and the meadowlarks just sang their throats out!

"Whoa, take it easy, we're not in flight," says Rusty.

We eased off. Just a good brisk amble. Rusty was ever the unhurried rider. He was very easy on a horse.

"If you have to spur your horse you better get another horse," was one of his oft-spoken remarks. If men were as good to one another as Rusty was to a horse the world would be a better place to live in. You'd never see him ride much more than an hour but he'd dismount and reset his saddle, loosen and regirth, run his hand under the cinch. And he'd take a good look at the country, both forward and where he'd been. If he saw something you'd know by the twitch of his eyes.

We climbed up from Goose Creek valley and were hours on end crossing the divide; then it was the flats, where we dismounted and let our hind ends cool. We took the bits out and let the horses eat for a while. Not too much, though, because this was the side oats grama grass which they weren't used to. You had to be especially careful at that time of year and watch out for the bloat. Then we remounted and he had a good, long look; and I did, too, but all lay serene under the heat wave.

"See anything?" he asked.

"Nope." But I know that *he* had. Rusty was possessed of the most marvelous eyesight, which was also in good part knowing how, and reading sign, such as the soar of birds, and the sort of flicker in the mirage; it was having the *feel* for it, which I hadn't, taking after Ma's side of the family. "What is it?"

"Oh, nothing special, but we'd better split up. Like you told the Brigadier, I like to sleep alone in the moonlight. Ride alone, too. Ha-ha! Don't want all the Irons killed in one volley. Ha-ha-ha! Meet you at the old Stamp place. All right?"

So we parted ways.

"Don't ride close to any gullies!" he called.

Gosh all willikers, I knew that much!"

I rode and rode, all by my lonesome. It was fairly hot, but not too. We always have a wind in that high country. The ground had scarcely a stone, all soft gumbo with grass and low sage that whispered underfoot. There's something marvelously fine about riding free, letting your horse just pick his way, and is the reason men choose cowboying, would rather have it than any other life, despite the hardships, the dangers and poor pay. The mind is free to roam, and mine got to roaming onto Rusty and Grace. Was he heading someplace to meet her? One thing I knew, he hadn't struck out for the old Stamp place. It was more like the old Donovan house. (I say "old" because both were abandoned. Most of the early ranches were abandoned, sold to the big cattle outfits.) After a time my horse smelt water. So away we went at a jingling clip down to the ponds, all cattails and greenery, and nesting mallards, on Donovan Creek. I was lying on my stomach having a drink when *pop!* something which sounded like a gunshot.

I lifted myself and listened. It was so quiet I could hear the water as it dripped off my chin. Then *pop* I heard another. It was a flat sound, no echo, due to the heavy noon heat.

It might have been Rusty, signaling. However, he wouldn't be likely to use the second cartridge. What he'd do was fire once and then raise a halloo. More like it was somebody shooting at him. They could have dropped him with the first and finished him off with the second; they'd have just about the time to ride up.

Minutes passed. I mounted and rode up the creek, slowly, you can bet, hunting the few box elder trees. I had no rifle, remember, only my six shooter. And it wasn't the best. It was a Colt, .45 calibre, six inch barrel, but it had only cost me $3 because the ratchet was worn and wouldn't align. You had to do it each time with your thumb, and not shake it when you fired or else it would (a) misfire, or (b) shave off a silver of lead, and also kick so as to almost tear your arm off. No gunfighter's piece, surely, but for all that I'd rather stand behind it than in front of it.

My course took me up behind more sloughs, with all the dead stuff and trees, to where I could see the house. There were three riders. Three on horseback and one man walking. The man afoot was Rusty. This gave me some relief, but not too much, unknowing what they had in mind.

I tied Old Brindle in the thickest bushes I could find and went on afoot. Sometimes I took off my boots and waded, and again I skulked and crawled, around cattails and sedge, and behind sagebrush to some downstream sheds, fallen corrals, etc., where I daren't go further.

They were all gone from view. They were on the other side of the house. It was the only place they could be. I saw Rusty's horse with the reins trailing, away off. I waited and waited. Beyond the sheds was a root cellar and cache house, and a scaffolding of two posts and crossmember where beefs had been pulled for butchering. They would shoot them, and pull them up hind first, and cut their throats to bleed. The grass there grew thick and green, reminding you of old buffalo kills.

All of a sudden here they came! Three men on foot, marching right along. Army style. One was Rusty. He walked strange, but soon I see it was on account of his hands being tied in front of him. They were buckled, actually, with a mail strap off a saddle. It was one of the neat touches you learned to expect from the Brigadier. He was, follering with a rifle in the crook of his arm. The other man had a coil of rope. And, oh God! my heart going sick inside me, they were headed for the beef scaffold!

The man with the rope was "Whip" Cotton, the Brigadier's range boss. He went under the scaffold where he fastened a piece of wood in the noose and tossed it up and over. He got it swinging where it suited him and tied to a post. The Brigadier led Rusty up facing it.

I had not the slightest doubt they were going to hang him. The one thing missing was the drop. I had never seen a man hung, but had heard about it numberless times, and they always had a barrel, or an old wagon, or they sat him on the rump of a horse. The Ringbone Kid said the latter makes the best of all drops because a horse when scared makes a little hop, lifting the victim so he comes straight down and isn't carried forward to swing; he said it causes the neck to snap every time. This all came back in sickening memory.

"Oh God, oh God, don't let 'em do it." I closed my eyes and prayed as hard as I was able. "Oh, blessed Jesus, please don't let them. Grant me this and I'll never ask another favor, ever!"

What I'd have to do, with Jesus' help, was try to sneak up with my old pistol and try to bluff them. To be truthful, I was more scared of Cotton than the Brigadier. He was the sort of man who never backed off from anything. The Brigadier might decide his own life was too valuable for the chance, but not Cotton once he made up his mind.

Well, when I opened my eyes I see Cotton wasn't putting the noose around Rusty's neck, but around

42

his wrists! He made a figure-eight and stepped back to get the other end of the rope and haul him up. It took all his might. Whilst the scaffolding creaked, Rusty was pulled up arms high and stretched out, toes barely on the ground. I could tell it was causing him quite a lot of pain because he was cursing them, calling them the worst kind of names, and I wished he would stop, but little did it bother the Brigadier! Oh, he was *cool!* He held his cigar. He smoked the thin, panatela shape. He stood just like he had that day at Steele when his daughter got off the stage. You couldn't have told the difference, he was so in command. Maybe both sights were equally satisfying to him. He must have told Cotton to go back to the house: "Get out of sight and keep the others out of sight," he must have said. "This here's a private matter between Irons and me." Because that's what happened. He took his time and took his time. He took off his coat, folded it, and laid it down. He turned up his cuffs, fastening the links. God, he was deliberate! He took from his belt a cow whip and rolled it out, snap!

"Irons!" he says. His voice had that parade ground ring. "Irons, I could in all justice have you shot. I could have you shot like a cur and not a decent person in the land would blame me."

I don't know if Rusty answered.

"There's one reason I don't have you shot, and one only. I don't want your carrion befouling my daughter's name."

He walked around, testing the whip. As I said, it was a cow whip, hence shorter than a bull whip, but with a longer and thicker tongue. He wanted it to roll out just so. Finally he seemed to be satisfied. He took a look at the house, a good long one, making certain. Then here it came, out and around, and *whap!* The sound was late, because of the distance. Sound travels five counts to the mile. You see the smoke rise from a shot, and count to five with deliberation, and *pop!* Well, this was about one count. I heard Rusty sort of squeal from the surprise and pain, and he went to his knees making the scaffolding weave. All this to the Brigadier's satisfaction. He had a puff, and stroked his moustache, and had another swing with the cow whip.

Whap! it goes again. "E-e-e!" goes Rusty.

"Take it like a man!" says the Brigadier.

Rusty cursed him, and *whap!* went the whip again. He was very slow. He was making it last. He wasn't going to blister his palm, and so dried it on a handkerchief. *Whap!* and "E-e-e!" Rusty would cry out, through nostrils and clenched teeth.

"Whining won't help. What your kind needs is a stretch in the Army. Discipline makes men." And he repeated, "Men!" when he swung the whip once more. "Leave people to their own resources," (*whap!* goes the whip) "and you fail, fail." He says, "You're trash! Trash you start life and trash you finish!" (*Whap!*) And he kept saying, "Trash! Trash!" as he swung the whip.

Finally he paused. He looked at his palm, which was taking some abuse. Took out a white handkerchief to pad it. Gave Rusty one more lick, but he seemed to have tired of the apple. Subject such low-down trash as not to be worth it. Lit his cigar. Had a few puffs. Looked all around to make sure his men weren't peeking. Took out his clasp knife and cut the rope. It was a genuine linen lariat, plaited and oiled, over a rawhide core, a very good article, worth 10 cents per foot at any store, but he just whacked it off. Rusty didn't fall. He reeled around on his sea legs and

44

ended kneeling, hands still tied. The rope was fitted with a Mexican non-slip honda. The Brigadier reached with a toe and sort of loosened it. Gad! he was cool. Not one show of anger. An Army man to the bone, administering discipline.

Finally he walked off. I could see shadows moving beyond the house and at last they left, no parting backward glance, at least so far as I could tell. Later, much later, when they were clean gone, and I couldn't make out even the shapes of their horses, I ventured out to take care of Rusty who was sitting bent over, holding one of the posts, his head padded against it with his hat. He had been that way for a quarter hour and maybe longer, not making a move.

Chapter Four

O, Brignal banks are wild and fair,
And Greta woods are green . . .
                    —The Lady of the Lake

"**R**usty! It's me, Hank."
        I finally got him to crawl which helped limber up his arms, which had got pretty much out of joint at the shoulders.

"Where is he? Where is the foul son of a b- - -h?"

"He's gone. They all rode off."

I got him to lie in the cattail pond. The cool mud helped him. It soaked up his shirt and undershirt which were full of blood. Actually it wasn't so much blood, but an ooze that comes forth and turns into a sort of glue. Gad! did the flies like the smell of it! After I got his back bared they came absolutely avid, big brassy flies with their proboscises down. They settle and you'd have to actually scrape them off. You'd have to mash them with your fingers. Later I got him to lie and let me cover his back with wet pond weeds, moss, muddy duck brackle, and the like.

"Bring me a drink."

"Can I use your hat?"

"No, you can't use my hat!"

It was his expensive one, made to personal block,

and my own had holes in it, and was rank from sweat.

"You fool!" He cursed me, but I didn't mind. I was too glad to see him coming around to being his old self.

I found a sardine can and used that, making about ten trips. He fell asleep, so I got my horse and rounded up Flyer. They had left all his stuff—rifle, pistol, everything. When I got back Rusty felt well enough to sit and have a smoke. I had to roll it for him his fingers were so swollen, but he could hold it to his own lips.

"Did you see who they were?" he asked, eying me.

"Nope." I guessed he didn't want me to know, it was too demeaning to be whipped by a girl's parent. I figured he'd rather have it thought he was caught by the Freezeout Gang, or somebody.

"How'd you happen to find me?"

"I thought I heard some shots. Then I saw Old Flyer on the loose."

He regarded me. He wasn't the easiest person to fool. However, I'm a pretty fair liar. I have a way of acting stupid, and let my mouth sag. Also, he *wanted* to believe me.

"What happened?" I asked, continuing this charade.

"What the h- - - do you think happened?"

"Was it Hoffner and his bunch?"

"I have a good idea, but it's my affair."

"Were they masked?"

"I won't tell you anything because I want you to stay out of it. This is something I want to take care of myself."

Finally he said he was ready to ride. His back was too raw to stand the feel of a shirt, and the sun on his naked skin was even worse. What we finally did was cut a hole in the back of his shirt and he put it on capote style. We set out and the wind flowed under it, a fair arrangement.

"I don't want a word of this to Ma, understand?"

We weren't headed anywhere close to home, anyhow. We were riding toward noplace at all that I knew about. As I said, it was a fearsome big country, great reaches of it unknown even to a person like me who had been there since practically his first hour. You could look off across broken land at ranges of hills or mountains floating in a mirage. It would remind you of the heat rising from a stove where pancakes were cooking. Closer at hand was a place called the White Rims. These appeared to be hills, but were actually the prairie left in islands. It was the start of the badlands. The *Mauvaises Terres,* the French breeds called it, and there were places called *tetons,* little summits that looked like tits, with the cap rock like a nipple. That was what *teton* means, in French, or at least in "Coyotie French," which is the lingo these people speak. You found them still living down there, in hidden valleys. They trapped wolves, or got them by poisoning, and they chopped wood for the steamboats. You could see where the river ran, flashing here and there, miles away, winding around on itself. For about two hundred miles, as the crow flies, four hundred by boat, the passengers got a look at some of the wildest shores on earth, and it was still possible to be shot at by the Indians. "The Great Wolfhowl, Pa used to call it.

We follered one coulee after another, and it seemed like we were lost. "Hey!" I said, rousing Rusty. He looked bleary at me. "Where we going?"

"Trust me, little brother."

What else could I do? It came evening, too late to turn back. If you kept going long enough and down hill you had to get to the river. Sometimes you got to one of the sinks, or alkali lakes, but as a general rule water flowed to the river. There you could foller the bank and find a woodhawk's hut, or one of the landings. These were many, but for the main part abandoned. There would be a high bank facing deep water where the steamboats could unload, but in a couple of seasons the banks might cave in and all you had were mud islands. Every kind of thief and outlaw lived down there because you couldn't find a sheriff or Federal Marshal who would venture to go in after them. Roads went down, too, and there were regular towns. The Army maintained a road from Toll Landing ("Fort McKibbin") to the Goose Creek Ranch, all the way to Castle Rock and the main stage road from Fort Steele to Judith, Castle, Diamond City, Helena, etc. If by now you feel lost, join the fraternity! Cowboys, badlanders, trappers, even the wild Indians, would get lost and wander to their doom. I have it on good authority there are still buffalo in the bad lands, and skeletons are found of animals sixty feet long, but prehistoric, long before man's dominion.

(While on this subject, I must mention the Hole in the Wall, and the so-called Hole in the Wall Gang. The Hole in the Wall Gang, if there ever was any *one* such, rather than several, stole horses in Dakota, and even in Minnesota, and drove them by way of the river all the way to the gold camps, or even to Idaho. They could travel the entire distance from Dakota to Fort Benton, head of navigation on the river, and never come out of the bad lands once. The Hole in the Wall was their storied hangout. It was a place where they simply rode up to a blank cliff and *vanished*. That was the story.)

There were bad lands on the north side of the river, too, but we let the Indians worry about them. It was the Reserve of the Piegan Blackfeet.

"Watch out for snakes," says Rusty, breaking my reverie.

Snakes were numberless, and evening was the worst time. They can cause your horse to bolt and leave you on the ground. You're not likely to be bit, but you sure can be left afoot. We turned up a side coulee which narrowed and steepened, and there was a crumbly footing. The moon rose. We rode around the side of a hill, and down a gully. You could tell it was clay dirt by how it filled the nostrils. I got to wondering if Rusty knew what he was about, because it kept getting worse, but we came down on some little flats, a coulee big enough to hold box-elder and bull-berries, a stream gone dry with washed-over pebbles, and the horses smelled water. We came to some old cottonwood stumps with saplings growing out of them. They had been taken out for a cabin, and some corrals. All was overgrown. There was a spring and a small stream.

"Whose place?"

"Mine. Ours. It can be our secret."

"You build it?"

"I fixed it up. Old man Honker told me of it."

This was "Goose" Honker, a wolfer who had died some years before. I recalled him well. He bragged to have never taken a bath, and Ma wouldn't allow him inside the house. Dad Marsh, down at the cook house, would feed him, but not at meal time, the men would complain. Goose thought it was real funny. One time the boys lassoed him and tried to haul him through the creek and spoil his record, but he got loose.

"Goose Honker keeps watch of his old place when I'm not around," said Rusty.

It was a joke, but it cast a chill through me, dark like it was, and so lonesome and still, the old cabin logs bleached like bone, and the window with its awful Stygian blackness.

"Don't even Ringbone and Preacher know of it?"

"No, just me, you and old Goose."

We drank, all four of us, Rusty, me and the two horses. The water was first-rate, not a touch of alkali. A sandstone spring. I unsaddled and picketed the horses whilst Rusty went inside.

"Got a match?" he asked from the blackness.

I did, and I knew he did, too, but was just too tired to scratch. I lit one and looked around. There was a bunk with hay in it, a table on a hinge that could be let down, and a sheet metal stove on clay bricks built half in and half out to emit smoke without need of a chimney. There was a grease lamp consisting of an old tomato can and wick. It was hung by a wire so the mice couldn't get to it and eat the bacon grease. Gad! I was hungry! I felt like eating that grease myself. We'd left without breakfast, remember, and had nothing since.

"Any grub around here?"

"No." He didn't sound like a man interested in food.

"Not even any beans?" People always had beans.

"No, not a thing. I like to live off the country."

There was a can for cooking. Two mice had fallen in and died. A long time previous—they were dry as leaves. I scoured the can intending to make tea of anything to be found. Red willow—actually the red-bark

51

dogwood—made a good tea and quieted the spirits, but it was too dark to hunt for.

"What in hell are you doing?" says Rusty. "Hold the lamp so I can look at my back."

He couldn't see a thing. His head wouldn't turn that far. He lay on his stomach and had me do it. It looked terrible, all welted and swollen.

"Ow! damn you," he yelled.

"How about a mud poultice?"

"No, just lay a wet shirt over it."

I did whilst he comforted himself with cigarettes, and he went to sleep. He was up and down all night, and as soon as daylight came I built a fire and made tea of kinnikinnick, old leaves and dried-out berries which I found on the slope. It's not much like tea, but it has a wild and spicy spirit which dries the mouth and kills hunger. Take enough and you get visions, but I was a long way from that. Rusty drank his cool and smoked and smoked; he must have smoked twenty cigarettes in all; and I took the rifle to look for game.

Many deer tracks, but no deer. I found a sagebrush flat and shot two sage hens, very tough old birds and strongly flavored. When a man is starving he can always kill either a sage hen or a porcupine, both being slow and very stupid. Given a choice most people will take porcupine, to give you an idea of what our breakfast was to be like. I roasted the hens over coals, and tough though they might be, the odor nearly drove me crazy. But Rusty said,

"Take 'em away! Go outside and eat. It sickens me."

He was asleep on his stomach with head and arms hung over the bunk when I left to picket the horses on new grass; when I got back in about half an hour he sprang up with a wild look on his face and cried, "Who are you? What are you doing here?"

"I'm Hank, your brother."

"My brother was shot dead."

He must have thought I was claiming to be Cecil who was killed down in Wyoming.

"I'm Hank. Look at me."

"You're John Bartless."

It was a new one on me. I knew a John Bartlett but not a Bartless.

Then he said, "You're Dennis. Stay away from me."

I kept telling him I was Hank, and he says, "Hank, where's my gun?"

Fortunately he hadn't taken his pistol along, only the rifle, and as soon as I could I got it away and hid it.

"Where you been?" Rusty asked when I came back.

"Out tending the stock."

"You been talking with Dennis!"

"He isn't here."

"He was here. Now, where did that son of a b- - - go?"

I had to make up things to placate him. I pretended that Dennis had been there, but he had gone someplace.

"Maybe he went for the doctor. How do I know where he went? He never tells me anything."

"He went for the sheriff, that's what he did!" And so on, ever and anon, and it got very frightening when he took it into his head that I was dead. "Stay away. Don't you come near. You're dead and through no fault of mine."

I wasn't sure it was me supposed to be dead, or Dennis. He would sleep for about fifteen minutes, feverish, and every time wake up raving and lashing around. It was all I could do to hold him, and he scraped the scabs off. I was all smeared with blood. The best treatment was when he drank water. I went back and forth to the spring about a dozen times. But at last, at night, he dropped off into a very deep sleep, and I slept, too, and when he woke up next morning he was himself again.

"I had terrible dreams. What did I talk about?"

I told him about Dennis and Bartless, but he didn't explain, nor has he to this day.

"Did I talk about Grace?"

"Nope."

"Come on, now, honor up! What did I say?"

"Not a thing."

"You tell me what's good for me, don't you, little brother?"

"No, it's the honest truth. You never spoke her name."

The swellings went down and scabs formed. They oozed watery stuff which brought the flies, and I had to keep him bathed, pretty much all the time. He would lie and moan with pleasure. I never had felt so close to him, or more like he was my brother. Next day he was well enough to get up and around, wearing his shirt. He said the worst thing was the terrible itch. He had some salve at home and wanted me to get it. We could do with some food, too, being very tired of sage hen; and he wanted his chaps, clean clothes, a folder of documents, mail, tobacco, etc. He rode as far as the rims with me and promised to wait so there'd be no question I'd find my way back.

"Oh, thanks be to God!" Ma cried when I walked in. "I haven't slept more than an hour of a night, worrying."

She wanted to know everything, of course, and I gave her a correct version insofar as it went; and I got away again with the stuff, and found Rusty waiting, and this chapter in the history of the Irons family ends.

Chapter Five

The extreme strength of the country, however, with the numerous passes, marshes, caverns, and other places of concealment or defense, made the establishment of this little fort seem rather an acknowledgement of the danger than an effectual means of securing against it.

—Rob Roy

O ut of the blue Rusty says, "Little brother, how'd you like to visit the famed Hole in the Wall?"

As you recall, I made a special point in telling about this strange phenomenon in the preceding chapter. For good reason, because it was to figure very importantly in my life, in fact on it hinged life itself.

Naturally, I jumped at the chance. Freshly horsed, rested and healed we rode down Cottonwood Creek to Uncle Will's homestead cabin and then across the grain of the country into a jumble of big, bald-face hills, many carved into harsh and forbidding shapes, to look for fossils. Rusty knew considerable about these strange remains of a bygone age since he'd tended the horses on Prof. Seely's celebrated expedition of '76, a year previously mentioned in re the Custer fight, when Pa moved us to Benton for safety. Once news came of what the Sioux had done to Custer the River Crows, Gros Ventre, Piegans and the rest went on the war hoot, shooting at steamboats, etc., but Prof Seely kept right on digging, and in fact made friends with the Indians, who called his fossils *devil horses.* Rusty told of one instance when Prof. Seely took out his false teeth and scared the living daylights out of them, they thought he was taking his head apart.

Much has been made of reptiles seventy feet long and fearsomely fanged, but there were many smaller creatures including the prehistoric horse, or *equs,* which was but three feet high. This was all set forth in a series of articles in the *Chicago Herald,* weekly edition, which we read with avid interest to see if Rusty got mentioned, which he did, twice. Rusty was quite an authority and had read Darwin's book on evolution, which he'd borrowed from a lawyer. He said the *euis,* or "dawn horse" was proof positive, being a lesser stage, other links being known down in Wyoming, link after link across millions of years, right up to the present, but Ma said it was nothing of the kind, they were simply those animals that hadn't been taken into the Ark and were drowned. Preacher Harlow, a friend of Rusty's, and a suspected cattle rustler, said likewise: that so far from proving the Darwin theory of evolution it knocked it into a cocked hat. They engaged in terrible arguments about this, and whether man had come from monkey, and one time the Preacher got so mad he grabbed a singletree and chased Rusty all over the yard yelling, "I'll learn you a thing or two! Make sport of the Holy Word and I'll learn you with a club!" Rusty leading him a merry chase: "Remember the Golden Rule! Turn the other cheek!" etc.

I tended to agree with Rusty on *most points*, and Pa

did, too. Pa said he'd rather be descended from monkeys than from most of the people he'd heard about in the Scriptures, but no mention of this before Ma because we wanted to keep peace in the family.

So much for that. We found a fossil skull Rusty already knew about, and some leaves of the giant fern, and killed two rattlesnakes, and were some distance down a dry river valley when Rusty pulled up and said, "All right, little brother, let's see you find our way out."

I follered our tracks for a while but lost them in the rocky going. Everything looked different going back. All was new scene. And Rusty, smirking.

"Let this be a lesson to you. Never go into new country without leaving a *sign*."

"I didn't have a chance. You never stopped."

"You don't have to, nor get off your horse."

"Did you leave a sign?"

"I did."

I couldn't figure out what unless he'd dropped something as he rode.

"Keep looking. It's right under your nose."

It turned out to be a cigarette paper that he'd folded and stuck in the top of a sagebrush. A person would never notice it unless he was looking for that one particular thing, and when he did it stood out like a *banner*.

"See how it adjusts to the wind?" said Rusty. "It turns like a weathercock; hangs tight through storm, rain, snow. Genuine French paper. Next summer you come past here and there it'll be. Now, look around. Can you see anything else?"

I couldn't, of course, and he pointed to a twig right on top he'd broken and left dangling by its tough bark never to be noted unless you were looking, and next he burnt off a twig leaving a black stub, extremely durable.

"Never leave an empty cartridge, the magpies will carry anything off that's bright. If you want to mark a place permanent, don't mount a stake, water will float it off. Dig a hole about one foot deep and build a fire in it and that black spot will remain through the ages."

"What if a flood comes and all gets worshed away?"

"Not *worshed* away, washed away."

Ma always said *worshed,* so I did, too. Rusty spoke different every time he came back from somewhere. He'd meet with Grace and not only smell different, but sound different.

"Learn all this from the Indians?"

"No, from the surveyors. They use charcoal pits to mark corners when there's no wood or stone for monuments. The Indians aren't so guided. They are more guided by the sky. The stars are their compass and the moon their calendar. Coming home after following the buffalo. Before the country went to hell."

He sounded like Pa. Neither liked cattle. They raised cattle because it was where the money was. Both were horsemen, not herdsmen. They put up with cattle, but they loathed sheep. "I like me beef on a plate and my sheep in a coat," the horsemen used to say.

Back to the badlands and the signs thereon:

"Never try and make charcoal out of sagebrush. It turns gray as cigar ash. Spanish bayonet the same. Pine knot is good, or juniper. Willow makes a good char. Biscuits make good charcoal."

He was sure worth listening to when it came to the lore of the wilds. I wouldn't fancy the task of catching Rusty in the badlands.

The country kept getting bigger and steeper. On the

high cliffs there were eagles' nests. These looked like bundles of sticks. You might not even see them, even standing out as they did, but for the droppings which made long swipes like whitewash from a brush of the gods. You never saw an eagle come to rest, however. They would fly along the cliffs and disappear.

Although early the season, none of the watercourses were so much as damp. I was parched for a drink. Of course Rusty would take no water. He figured a man ought to drink when his horse did, because it was up to the two to come through together. I noticed Old Hazel jerk and get her head up.

"Smells water."

"Not here she don't."

"Tell it to Hazel!"

"You take the word of that old mare before your brother?"

She led us up an unlikely way, steep and rocky. Rusty just marveled! "She's right!" he says, happy as could be. It always pleased him to be proved wrong by a horse. "By the God, I think there's water in there!"

It was all brushy under the rims, with fallen rock and slot caves. One layer of sandstone is never quite the same hardness as another, hence the softer tend to wash away and caves develop. These are great places for animals such as skunks and bobcats. We crawled away in, and sure enough, there was damp coolness and the music of water. It wasn't something you could actually hear, more like *feel*, like you feel the sound when somebody runs his thumb nail along the E string of a fiddle.

Water dripped from a hundred stones and ran off through crevices. You could catch it in your hand, or hold your hand up and lick it off your elbow. We caught it in our hats and carried to out to the horses, innumerable trips. After we were finished Rusty went around with a switch, cleaning away all sign of us being there.

"Why keep it hid?" I asked. "Why not put up a sign reading 'water' and maybe save some person's life?"

"That's one way of looking at it," he says, "but just as a matter of principle, when you know something that other people don't, why, it could be to your advantage. It's a dog-eats-rabbit world."

Dog may eat rabbit, but we ate nothing. Taking food along was not Rusty's style, no more than was water. Just tobacco and papers. If your horse can stand it, you can, was his oft remark.

"Yes, but a horse carries his own tank of food and water," I thought of saying. "And they get water from browse." Which is true. A horse can get by on shrubs, watery legumes, etc. hardly any water at all. However, I didn't argue. He couldn't stand argument. Only from friends like Preacher Harlow and Lucius Engate, "The Ringbone Kid." We slept on horse blankets, head against saddles. Cold even in that summer season. Cold crept up from the river and down from the hills. We could hear our horses moving about. He always cross-hobbled, didn't trust a picket rope. "You may have to walk half a mile for a hobbled horse, but ten for one on a rope, if he gets loose." I could hear them in the dark, grazing, the rip-rip as they tore off the grass. And if there was the slightest thing amiss, a pause. Stop. His horse is the best sentry your cowboy has.

We got up to a dry, hungry camp and found our horses practically waiting to be saddled. We had taken the precaution of sleeping in the midst of the very best pasture, which is another in your cowboy's bag of tricks. With no breakfast to worry about we were soon on our way. Rusty smoked cigarettes one after the other, killing the want for food, though I could see that getting spit enough to lick the paper was a problem. And when finished down to the stub he would have to peel them off his lips where they got glued. We were in a monstrous watercourse, big enough to hold some mighty Missouri, but dry as a bone. We climbed out of it by way of a gully exactly like a dozen other gullies, thence to some shoulder ground, a crenelated prairie, narrow slots you had to watch out for, lest your horse break a leg, and Rusty would say each and every time, "Horse meat for supper!" and pretty soon we were climbing slowly, toward a long reef of sandrock. This was one of the mountain ridges you could see from our home ranch, looking north, where the setting sun gleamed.

It shrank, seemed to get lower as we approached. What looked like a solid wall broke into spurs and crevices. There was much fallen stone, blocks from the size of cookstoves up to small cabins. Some of those slabs must have weighed a hundred tons. A trail appeared and led us in and around. There were tracks of game, deer droppings. Then a breeze, blessed cool. Couldn't imagine where it came from. It was like a spring of cool water flowing from solid rock. Another zig and zag, a last little pitch, and that stone wall opened right before us! It just parted at the final second, a gash that might have been cleaved with the axe of the gods.

"This is it!" says Rusty.

"This is what?"

"Why, the Hole in the Wall!"

What I'd pictured was an actual hole, like a tunnel. "What's on the other side?"

"A valley. The famous hideout."

"Holy smokes! Is anybody there?"

"That's what we'll find out."

He was cautious. So were our horses. I thought for a while we'd have to get off and lead them, maybe even blindfold, because they'd never been in such a place, not even inside a barn, no place except under the open sky. However, the roof wasn't all solid. There were crevices where at times you could see the sky, a very deep blue. Went in and out and up and down, with a couple of tight turns and came out in the sunshine on a pocket valley, or basin. Fallen stone was even worse than the other side, far more extensive, a regular devil's orchard. There was a great deal of brush—skunkbush, squaw current in bloom, and at a distance the rounded shapes of buffalo berry trees. More cliffs. "A cirque," said Rusty, something he'd picked up from Prof. Seely.

We started down. No trail. It was so steep your horse went right to its haunches, but you were well advised to stay in the saddle, not go out ahead, because you might get stomped on. Never place yourself so you'll get a horse on top of you. That's a cardinal rule in the hill country.

"Dead Man's Basin," said Rusty, at a pause.

There were several Dead Man's Basins, a common enough name.

"And that is the Iron Wall," pointing to some black hued cliffs. "Manganese stain. About one pound of manganese will color the side of a mountain. You can say the same for copper, but it gives peacock hues. Iron stain is always red. The paintbrush of Mother Nature. The river lies over there, about six miles, but you'd never make it. Break-leg country."

"If it's a basin there must be water. I'm parched!"

"There's an alkali sink, some sort of yellow sul-
phone."

"How do the deer get by?"

"Have to ask them, little brother."

However he took pity on me and said there was a
spring, if it hadn't dried up, in which case we would
have to dig.

There was a great deal of big sage in the bottom,
and it must have been the cactus capital of the West.
Prickly pear. Also button cactus. No blossoms as yet.
We came to a dry stream bed and this led to the sink
which smelled not unlike a pickle vat. The horses
turned from it, water was that bad. Mainly mud with
yellow edge. You could see the bones of animals that
had ventured too close to their ancient doom.

We rode around it, using care, because often the
ground will seem perfectly dry and safe, and suddenly
give way and suck you down, and a rider can save
himself only by jumping clear. I already mentioned
the buffalo berry trees. Also called bullberries, or, by
the Texans, gumbullos. Red berries in the fall, make
the finest of jelly. These grew strictly on dry shoulders
of ground. About a quarter mile away I could see some
quaking ash, or aspen, which constitute a much better sign of water. And, sure enough, we came to the
spring, a large area of trodden mud, with cold water
stirring here and there, and running from one track to
another.

"Not too fast," says Rusty. Gad, I knew that much!
A person can kill himself by drinking with crazy
thirst. Took it easy, resting, and drinking again.
Caught a frog and ate it. I was that hungry. Rusty
laughed and laughed. "You just have to make up your
mind. Used to go without food for three days. Indians
do it all the time."

There was a good enough cabin, small but solid, and stumps where long ago the logs had been cut. Also a corral. He showed me a grave neatly marked by stones. This gave me the shudders, and the feeling as of secret eyes watching, so I was glad enough when he says,

"Show's over! Let's get out of here. You lead the way."

I couldn't do it! I backtrailed easy enough but lost out on the steep going. I tried giving Hazel her head. Mares are supposed always to head home, but she liked the place fine and cropped fresh shoots. I looked and there sat Rusty, grinning. Was he happy at my discomfiture! I'd have paid $5 out of purse to find that trail, but no use.

"Didn't you leave a sign? What have I been telling you?"

"How could I? I never had a chance."

"*Always* leave a sign."

"You never!"

"Don't be too sure."

That's a fact, I couldn't be. But more likely he had an old mark from seasons ago. This proved to be the case. He let me hunt for another quarter hour but he got impatient and says,

"Look above you, away up high on the rocks. I'll show you three landmarks. One is that drift of dead-wood."

Yes, I'd noticed it. It was as if trees had grown there ages past and had died and washed down.

"Now, see that red splash? Recall what I told you about iron stain? I don't talk just to hear myself, little brother!"

"Yes, I see it."

"With both in view you walk until you see a ragged

65

pinnacle that looks like an old leg bone sticking up. Just keep moving. Get over here about fifty yards. Just keep traveling along. Here, now. All ought to be equidistant. Just like a gunsight. Now you ride straight out. Otherwise you'll be trapped in here forever."

It was a true blind pass, but that about being trapped in there forever seemed to be a bit extreme. I could have climbed out, though at the cost of leaving my horse. Hole in the Wall, well named!

That night we rode back to Hazel's Springs—our name for them—and next day back to Goose Honker's cabin. Rusty showed me where we could leave messages for each other between two of the logs, sort of our private mailbox down in the badlands, and the next day we parted and I went back home.

Chapter Six

"Ha! Pasques-dieu, Sir Squire,
methinks you keep sleepy ward here!"
                    —Quentin Durward

Ma was raging mad when I got there. Not at
me—she was too thankful to have somebody
to listen—but it seems that during my absence Hoffner had come around to argue water rights.

"Oh, was he all honey and goose grease! But the
threat was there!"

"Didn't he make some sort of offer?"

"He offered to relieve us of debt. What an insult! As
if we hadn't always paid our debts! He said he'd co-
sign as a favor. It was a plain and simple ruse to put us
in his power. 'You covet our range!' I told him. 'No,' he
says, 'I do not covet your range! In fact, Enterprise
has protected your range against encroachment.' "

"He had the nerve to say that?"

"Yes, he did. After all the time we spend driving his
cattle off! I said, 'You protect our range only so you
can grab it yourself.' 'No, Mrs. Irons,' he says, 'that's
not true. You don't seem to realize what's happening
in this territory. The cattle census doubled the year
after the Northern Pacific line was built, and is dou-
bling again. We'll have to unite or they'll overrun us
all.' 'Who'll overrun us all?' I says. 'Why those other

brands, the new ones.' 'They're not what I see on our range. What I see are the multitudinous brands of Enterprise Land and Cattle, Incorporated!' I told him. 'We shot the Indians off and we shot the buffalo off, and we'll shoot the Eastern corporations off if we have to!' " Then she got around to asking, "Where *you* been?"

"I had to go some places with Rusty."

"Where is he now? Is he chasing that girl again?"

"Not as I know of."

I guess there was no word of the whipping, though an encounter like that is impossible to keep secret forever.

Ma gave it to Rusty pretty hard for a while, dredging up a lot of his old failings, but finally she ran down and it was good to get home. Ellis Thrift and I took the wagon and went up in the hills for firewood, and I rode for strays, etc.; and one day I met Preacher Harlow, the Ringbone Kid—both bosom friends of Rusty's—and a stubby cowboy named Keg Williams.

"Where's Rusty?" asks the Preacher.

"That's what I was about to ask you."

"He was over in Castle the last I heard. I thought maybe he'd come home."

"Nope."

"Somebody has been spying on your home ranch, you know that?"

"Nope."

"Keg saw him, twice."

"Not exactly," said Williams, "what I saw was the flash from a spy glass."

"Where was it posted?"

"Right at the old buffalo jump."

"Did you prowl around up there?"

"Not me! I ain't lost any ambushers."

"Tell Rusty, will you?" says the Preacher. "You know what happened to your pa."

"I know."

These worthies had been waiting for me, not wanting to come to the ranch because Ma never made them welcome; she liked the Preacher all right, but she despised Ringbone, who had a very bad reputation; she considered him a bad influence on Rusty.

I said nothing of what they'd told me but decided to go up there and snoop around—not by day, I might get shot, but at night so I'd be posted at dawn to see who showed. Chose to ride old Moxler, a gray white gelding, very good at night. I mean not only did he have a nose for badger holes in the dark, but he was hard to see. Contrary to belief it's a white or gray and not a black which is hardest to spot after dark. Certain dapples are almost invisible. Leastwise that's true on the plains: they tend to blend with the ghostly sky, and with the sagebrush.

I didn't expect anybody to be there. Your ambusher is of a lazy breed. He seeks comfort not found in a fireless camp. It was a fine night, but cold, all the stars twinkling, not a sound. As stated, this was an old buffalo jump. It was a place where the Indians drove buffalo off and killed them. You could dig down and find hair and arrowheads. The cliffs over which the thundering herds were driven were not high—twenty foot at most. There were hollowed places where you could sit out of rain or sun. When one was cut by a gully you had a keyhole draw. I located one and made myself comfortable. I kept dozing and waking, waiting for dawn, fell fast asleep. I woke with a start in bright day. The sun had been up an hour, warming the broad land.

I realized that something had awakened me. I got

my rifle and sat quiet. What it was was a stirring in the bushes. It came and went, came and went, and of a sudden a big red dog burst through and looked at me.

"Woof!" he goes.

"Here, boy." He was afraid of the rifle so I put it aside. You can always tell when a dog has been shot over. He was looking not at me, now, but at something else. Somebody was above me. I froze right there.

"Hello!" says a girl's voice. It was Grace McKibbin! And the dog was one of her father's red retrievers.

She was standing right at the edge, and the sun was behind her. She was garbed horsewoman-style: boots, a riding skirt that came to the calf, and blue blouse and neckerchief; a flat brim hat was pinned on her hair.

"You're Hank, aren't you?"

"Uh-huh."

"I'm Grace McKibbin."

This was the first time we had spoken, though it seemed like I'd known her for a long while. She had a beautiful voice—it was so gentle and kind. The tone of it stirred one to the core.

"Gr-r-r!" says the retriever.

"Duke, stop that!"

He came up then and smelled my hand and we were friends from that time forth.

"Did you stay here all night?"

No good lie occurred to me so I said, "Yes. I was watching for you."

"For me?"

"Well, I heard somebody was spying from the rims."

"Yes, I've been here before. I've been watching for Russell."

"Haven't we all!" says I, fervently.

"Then you don't know where he is?"

"Nope. He never tells us much. He's a free soul."

I could see she didn't exactly believe me is why I added that last.

"I have to find him! I really do. It's very important." She seemed just simply desperate, and almost ready to cry. Well, I'd have done anything for her. "Do you know how I can, Hank?"

I had vowed that old Honker's cabin would be our secret and ours alone, but I figured she was a special case, so I said, "I do know one place he might come where we leave messages for each other."

"Do you? Will you take me there? Please?"

I had dug myself in too deep to get out. It was my history with that girl from then forward. All she had to do was ask. I'd have died for her.

"It's half a day's ride. More'n that from here."

I figured she'd say no, that was out of the question, because she'd have to get back home, but she didn't. I got my stuff and led old Moxler around and up to the rims. She not only had a dog, and a horse, but the horse was a mare with a colt at her side. A beautiful chestnut, typical of the McKibbin horses, finest in the land. It struck me as strange she would ride all that way with the colt at side, still in the suckling stage, but perhaps it allayed suspicion. Anyway, such a colt travels pretty well because he gets to eat and its mother doesn't.

"Give me a boost," says Grace.

"Upsy-daisy!" says I.

She needed a little boost because she didn't want to hoist her skirt to reach for the stirrup. It showed how wrong Ma was about her immodesty in riding astraddle.

We rode and rode, very hot, not a cloud, and fate took us right down on the old Donovan Ranch with its fatal beef scaffold; and right at that moment she said, "Why hasn't Russell met me? He was supposed to meet me the evening you left the ranch."

I knew it! I knew he had something set up. But that wasn't what jolted me. It was her asking at the very time we caught sight of the scaffolding. It was just as though she had a premonition. People do have them and it's called second sight. I'm not superstitious, or believe in mind reading or mesmerism, but it really gave me a strange and eerie feeling. You must remember that this was shortly after the Mother Shipton excitement about the world coming to an end. She lived at the time of Henry VIII, and had predicted many events; later they found her testament setting the end of the world for 1881, and a woman in Chicago burnt all her money, ten thousand dollars worth, in order to cleanse herself for the Second Coming. Hence my eerie feeling.

"Hank, what's wrong? What aren't you telling?"

"Nothing, he was tooken sick that morning we left your ranch. He was out of his head from fever." But I could see she didn't believe me. She knew there was something I was leaving out, so finally I just told her. "They follered him and your pa cow-whipped him."

"Papa *whipped* him?"

She went absolutely dead pale so I thought she might faint away, but she didn't. No, sir, not her! Not by a long shot. She got hold of herself and gave me a stare as hard as steel.

"Yes, he did," I said. "They caught up with him, your Pa, and Whip Cotton, and Tom Ward. Cotton drew him up by his hands on a lariat and went behind the house there, and your Pa gave him about forty lashes with a cow whip. I hid in the cattails and saw it."

I told her the whole thing, without exaggeration and without glozing over, and how we'd taken our long ride, and him being fevered and out of his head.

"Did he mention me—when he was out of his head?"

"No, it was all crazy. Mostly he saw visions and ranted."

"Oh." I wondered if she felt slighted, but more it seemed she was relieved. She had her color back, and then some! She was so angry her face simply shone! She wheeled around—we'd ridden all the way through the Donovan ranch yard—and came back, and looked at that scaffold, and was simply furious.

"Is that the rope?"

"Part of it. Your pa cut him loose and left it."

"And they just rode away?"

"They just rode off. I sneaked out as soon as I could. I put a poultice on his back. It was all whip cut. I had to keep off the flies. Rusty wouldn't let me go for help. He wouldn't go home, either. He just wanted to head into the badlands. He didn't want it known. He didn't even want me to know."

"It was noble of him. He's noble, noble, noble! It shows the kind of a man your brother truly is!"

Noble wouldn't have come to my mind for Rusty, but I said, "He's a real honest-to-God man, all right."

"Oh, Hank, I love him so!" She stopped right there and grabbed hold of my hand. "We're going to get married. No matter what Papa or anybody else says."

Married and what then? Where were they going to live? I'd be sorry for her moving in at our place, Ma feeling about her the way she did. They could hardly live in the old harness shed where Rusty put up. And living at the McKibbins' was out. If something happened to the Brigadier it might be worked out with Stanhope, and Grace would inherit a share. However, Rusty would never live off a woman. They'd have to go away, but there again Rusty knew nothing except cowboying. He knew how to survive in the wilds, but the wilds was not the place for a married man, except if he married a squaw. He had his estray business, and he made big plans. He toiled not, neither did he spin, Ma said. He had tended bar, and he told me once about something that happened when he was case keeper and lookout on a faro game. He'd managed the livery stable in Diamond. But you can imagine how those kinds of employment would set with a McKibbin!

"Where you going to live?"

"Some place far, far away."

Easy enough for her to talk, she with a parent that paid her train fare all the way to Ohio, and fees for a fancy girls' school, and pin money for her to come back unbidden in the drag days of winter.

"Russell talks about going to the Coast," she said, "Oh, there are just oceans of opportunities. I'd like to go to Alaska! I'd like to go on my own little boat."

I could see they'd been discussing it.

Chapter Seven

What sent the messengers to hell
Was asking what they knew full well.
—Highland ballad

As it turned out we didn't ride down to the badlands that day. It was too late. We agreed to meet three days hence and look for Rusty. Her father was gone, Stanhope was at the ranch, and Mrs. Skinner spied on her, but she said not to worry, she could handle *her.* We went, I found my way all right—no Rusty. I showed her our secret mailbox and she left a note for him.

I told her Rusty was sure to be home soon, he never missed, it was branding time, and Rusty would be on hand with a saddlebag full of vouchers from people he represented in his estray business, but for once I was mistaken. No Rusty. It left our ranch very short because we were obligated to furnish five men for the roundup, and we needed reps (representatives) at the Big Dry and Judith associations, too.

"I'll saddle and ride myself," said Ma.

She didn't, actually, but she showed up in the buggy. I went to the Big Dry, and then a hundred mile to the Judith, claiming stock at both, and how many we lost I'll never know. Home again, I was down in the lower pasture digging post holes when a short, heavy-set, oily visaged man rode up on a black gelding.

"Howdy," he says.

"Howdy," I answered.

"This the Irons place?"

"Yup."

"You Irons?"

"One of 'em."

"Rusty about?"

"Nope."

I must say right here I didn't like the way he sat and talked down at me. I don't mean a man has to dismount, though it's done in many instances.

"Where is he?"

None of your gol danged business, I felt like saying, but didn't. He was armed to the teeth and no witnesses.

"I don't know. He doesn't tell me anything."

"I was supposed to meet him. This is the Will Irons homestead?"

"It's below the fence."

"I'm Ben Butler."

He leaned over to shake hands, still on horseback.

"I'm one of his old friends. Ain't he mentioned me?"

"Can't say that he has."

He wasn't by himself. There was a second man skulking down the coulee, a small man with a miserable black hat. *Him* I had seen before. He was a one-time jockey named Crowfoot. The cattle were not your ordinary strays. They seemed to be a heavy beef stock, broad in the T-bone.

"What you got?"

"Come along and see."

They are cow thieves, thinks I, and what they stole

can mean plenty of trouble. Crowfoot says, "Hello, Irons," and I says, "Hello, Kid," because the men usually called him the Crow Foot Kid. "How's your Ma?" he asked, and I said, "Fine, how are your folks?" and they both seemed to think this was funny, but why I don't know.

The cattle were steers, heavy red three-year-olds with the Snake S, or Dollar brand, which I just chanced to recall by the charts on Rusty's wall as belonging to the J.T. Miller outfit, post office drawer Z, in Belle Fourche, Dakota.

"What's that, a Snake S?" I asked.

"Hey, what do you think of that!" yelled Butler. "He named it right off. There's an Irons for you!"

"I've repped a little," said I, feeling good. "But how in thunder did they get away over here?"

"Follered the river, I would guess."

"Their home range is the Little Missouri. They'd have to go north and double back again. Why, it'd be five hundred mile!"

It was plain, how would they have all that flesh on after such a stray? They'd be all torn and footsore. But they had an answer,

"According to Rusty," says Butler, "they were probably estrayed on the Assiniboine Reserve and got drove this way in revenge. Those Government Agents are truly mean. They been eating fat all spring all along the river."

It just could have been possible. It all squared with that Belle Fourche brand.

They were very put out that Rusty wasn't there to meet them; they'd driven all that distance through the rough country, no little feat; Crow Foot said they'd parted from him at the Coalbanks Ranch. This was quite a hangout for trappers, badlanders and other footloose types, and not a thing you'd brag about. How about the fee they'd been promised?

"I'll fetch Ma," says I.

Didn't have to. About that moment here she came, driving the buggy.

"What are those cattle? How'd the likes of you come by stock like that?" She was addressing Crowfoot. "You're a thief and a scoundrel!" she says. "You held back a horse at the Helena meet! You don't dare show your face!" etc.

They laughed and laughed, and Butler apologized for him; he said a man had to put up with all kinds of company, and then he set about telling her everything he had told me, but she cut him off.

"Those cattle were *stole!* I want 'em taken off our range promptly. If my son dealt for them, let him come in person and speak out!"

They argued and argued.

"If they had wintered on the river, why ain't their legs scarred by the ice?" etc.

However, when it turned out she could get them for a mere $3 each against what might be as much as $20 reward or empoundment fee, she eased off and said well, maybe they were strays after all; cattle *can* drift for hundreds of miles with the wind in their tails, and there *had* been a big, southeast blizzard the autumn before, and there *was* a lot of good grass along the river, untouched since the buffalo, etc., and the upshot was she paid over the money they asked. It was a foolish and risky thing to do. This became plain very soon.

"Now, I don't want to have a thing to do with those cattle," she said, "so you just leave them where they are, inside Uncle Will's homestead. They're your brother Russell's business, not ours. If he doesn't show up real soon we'll drive them to Castle."

As I said, Castle was the silver mining town with no-questions-asked market. It lay about two days drive to the west, just up from the Last Chance (Helena) road. Castle was an "island of easy money in a sea of hard work," was what Rusty said. They boasted about four butcher shops not a one of which cared a hang what brand was on a beef. They even destroyed the hides, which was illegal.

If we'd set off for Castle right away, the story might have been different, but we didn't, we stalled around, waiting for Rusty, and one morning—

"Henry! Get up!"

She was at the door with the Sharps rifle and riders were coming through the pasture and up and around, in what could only be called a military deployment. It was a very frightening thing to see.

"There's Monte Sallows!" which was a relief.

Sallows was the sheriff, an old friend whom Pa had one time saved from creditors when he failed in the freight business.

"It's him, but I don't like the looks of the company he chooses. Hoffner. Look how he rides. You'd think he owned the country. Henry, go out and see what they want."

It was a task I didn't relish. Don't know which bothered me the more, having to face that posse or having Ma at my back with her old Sharps rifle. This historic gun was a single shot .50 calibre, throwing a patched bullet weighting 480 grains, and capable of stopping a buffalo dead in its tracks. I sallied forth, picking up my six shooter, which was a mistake, and I realized it, but Ma says,

"Go on to the gate. Stand right there! This is our property," etc.

By now they were coming around the corrals and through the sheds. Actually there were only twelve men, but it was still quite a force for our country. Monte Sallows rode up, long and lank, black-hatted and black-moustached; and Hoffner; and I also recognized the undersheriff, Casey Hobbs, who was a bully; a part-time deputy named Lester Smith; Tex Mullens the Enterprise "detective"; Ed Peale and Long Henry Carmichael: mean characters all.

Monte Sallows, sheriff badge shining, sat and looked down on me like I was scum. He retched and made a terrible face, being afflicted always with the sour stomach, and he cried out, "What's that you're holding in your hand, you young whelp?"

Ma heard him and out she came. "That boy is at *home!* You're the one that rode in here armed. He's within his rights!"

I guess he didn't know she could hear him. "Thelma! There is no need for contention. Can I come in and talk with you?"

"Get your corporation gunmen off my place and you can!"

He didn't know what to do. He decided to have a swig of medicine. He whipped out a bottle just as if he was drawing a gun. Off came the cap and he swallered some. Either it tasted awful, or the thought of it was disgusting because with a curse he flung that bottle as hard as he could. It skidded off the ground and hit one of Ma's hens. The hen let out a cackle and went about two feet in the air. He couldn't have done it again in a hundred years, Wild Bill himself couldn't have with a gun. It was truly amusing. Some of the fellows laughed, but Ma was furious.

"What do you mean, coming here with your minions and killing a widow's chickens?" she yelled.

"It was an accident. You" he said to Tex Mullens, "go and fetch that bottle."

Tex, who was even taller than the sheriff, rode over and got it, did so without dismounting. He found the stopper, too. Not much had flowed out. For years Monte had taken Motherwell's Cascara, in the clear bottle, but this appeared to be something new, a squarish bottle and black.

"I rode all night, Thelma. I haven't been to bed in twenty-four hours." As if she had ought to feel sorry for him.

"Who are these men? Are they all deputies?"

"Yes, they are!"

"How about him?" she asked, meaning Hoffner.

"He's a citizen. He has a right to come."

Ma says to me, "Come back inside the house, Henry. We'll stand them off from here."

"No, you don't have to stand anybody off. Where's Rusty?"

"I don't know where he is."

"If you know where we can find him it would be best to say so."

"You got a warrant?"

"No, but I want to talk to him."

Others were pounding through the barn, the bunkhouse, Rusty's rooms, the old cache house, the root cellar. They had Ardis and Joe, the only cowboys there at the time, and soon they came with Dad Marsh, who was carrying his pants.

"Let that poor old man put on his clothes!" said Ma. "What's the trouble with you? Have you gone completely out of your minds?"

"He tried to get the drop on us!" a fellow said, and he was holding Dad's old needle gun.

"He was protecting his domicile!" Ma yelled.

"Take the cartridges out and give it back," said Monte.

Dad wouldn't take the gun when handed to him, however. He thought it was a trick so they'd have an excuse to shoot him. He sat down on the ground and put his pants on.

"I still ask where Rusty is."

"And I still tell you I don't know."

"Did he bring some steers here last week?"

"No, he didn't! I haven't laid eyes on him in near on a month."

This was approximately true. I had seen him but Ma hadn't.

"We have witnesses that he brought some steers here last week."

"There were steers brought, and legally, estrays, from Dakota, and by two men having no connection with this ranch."

"Where are these *Dakota* steers?"

He didn't need to ask. Here came some more riders driving the red steers, and they were under the command of Ed Wiggin, the brand inspector. They had really come loaded for us. Wiggin was a stocky, flashy sort of man, but I never had anything against him.

"Where'd you find them?" asked Hoffner.

"On the Will Irons homestead!" as if making a public pronouncement.

"Will you so testify?"

"I most certainly will."

Ma said, "They are *empounded.* They were off their *customary range!* You will move those steers at *your own risk!*"

82

I got into it, too, saying they were not even from the territory, but from Dakota, offering to show them the brand charts, the Snake S, also called the Big Dollar, being set down plain as day.

"We don't need any charts!" says Hoffner, and he told me to keep quiet until spoken to; when the brand inspector needed my advice he'd likely ask for it.

Wiggin wasn't too bad. He said he knew about the brand I talked about. He got in among the steers to feel of the brands to see if they were fresh burnt, and almost got hooked for his trouble. A horn grazed his eye and took his hat off. Then they tromped on it.

"Catch that steer and tie him down!" he yelled.

So Ed Peale shook out his lasso and worked around until he got the offender by the hind legs, both of them, quite a trick; it's easy to get one hind leg but you have to get them bucking to get two, and a fellow named Claude Bowers wrestled him down by the head, and they stretched him out tight as a drum while Wiggin had his look. He couldn't be sure, so others looked, and stood around with their brows wrinkled.

"I'm not sure, but it might have been burnt twice," said Wiggin.

"That's Tom foolery!" says Ma. "How can a body tell if it was burnt twice!"

"It's my business to know. It's how I earn my living." And he says, "Toss down another steer!"

So they did, and he examined it, and he stood up and says, "Mrs. Irons, I make no allegations, I trust you came by these cattle in a perfectly legitimate manner, but I'd say they were branded as calves and the old brands doctored probably with a point-iron since last fall. Come here and see for yourself."

Ma wouldn't deign to do so, but I did. "Looks just

like any old brand to me," and jeez! did he lose his temper!

"Leave that steer up!"

They did, and *bang!* Wiggin shot him. He shot him in the ear and down he went again, this time for good. He went heels over head deader than Dooley.

"Get his hide off!" says Wiggin.

They did, about five men at it, and had it peeled inside out in jig time, and Wiggin found where the brand was and had it scraped down. I'd never seen this performed, but I'd heard about it—what they do is take the skin down until the hair roots show and if there are separate scars, one old and one new, it can be determined. As was here the case. It wasn't a Snake S, it was an Anchor plain as day. This was a local outfit belonging to T.S. Gregory.

Ma talked a different tune, of course, saying she'd received in good faith from Ben Butler and The Crow Foot Kid.

"Did they sign a receipt?" asked the sheriff.

"No, but Hank heard them."

"They must have signed for the money."

"No, not with me."

"Did Russell pay them?"

"I don't know what he did. I don't know a thing about it. They could have been lying every step of the way."

I could see it looked very bad by how the sheriff snapped his memorandum book. He pulled me to one side.

"If you know where he is you better get him." Then he added very sotto voce, but in a tone that cast a bolt of fear right down my spine. "And make sure nobody follows you!"

Now, here is something you'll be hard put to believe. After all this they wanted to eat, and us to feed them!

"Where's your Western hospitality?" they asked.

But Ma went inside and they couldn't find our cook, Dad Marsh. He'd gone and hid. Hoffner said he was willing to dig up 50¢ each from his own pocket, and would I cook some bacon and eggs, and make coffee? But Monte Sallows said no, they would have to tighten their belts.

"Take that carrion with you!" Ma called, pointing to the dead steer, still warm and vapory, with flies circling over it. "Eat that why don't you?"

But they rode off. They took the hide for evidence, about fifty pounds of it, roped behind somebody's saddle. Soon all was quiet, and the song of the chickens was heard in the land.

Chapter Eight

Where then is the outlaw
Allan-a-Dale?

—Ivanhoe

"**I** want to know what Monte said to you," says Ma. "You turned as pale as whey."

It was no use lying. "He said I better find Rusty."

"He thinks you'll lead them to your brother. He wants you to be a Judas sheep."

"Hardly! He said be careful I wasn't follered."

The steer carcass was all flies, but the meat was perfectly good. We fell to and cleaned it up, the men helped, split it down the spine with the axe, and quartered it, and raised it high on some long poles. If you can get a beef to twenty feet in our windy climate the flies stop bothering, and the outside turns black and hard. It stinks to about one inch in depth and this can be peeled away, leaving the rest as sweet and tender as anybody could wish. It'll keep for weeks. The English do it all the time and call it "high bird." We saved out the heart, liver, sweetbreads, tripe, tongue, brains, kidneys, etc., which left little except scraps for the chickens. We had quite a feast that night, and next morning I set out to hunt for Rusty.

* * *

What I planned to do was head for one of the river ports such as Rocky Point or Cow Island and inquire around. There was no telegraph on the river, but word went back and forth by one means or another, so if he was around somebody would know about it. I set out carrying two sacks of food, some oats, a small keg of our famed Wildhorse Springs water, tarp, blanket, etc., and I borrowed one of Rusty's .44 calibre rifles. I rode Old Brindle, my favorite, and led a sorrel named Flick that Ardis Cribb had recently broke. The sorrel led better than he rode, but he would gentle down. When traveling far, into the wild country, it is a mistake to take all gentled stock. In this case the gentle one would keep the wild one around, whilst the wild one will help the gentle move into strange terrain— hence you have the best of both worlds.

I wish to set down here our legal situation as it will give some idea why we were so worried about Rusty.

Our territory (Montana) had recently passed a Livestock Commissioner Law for the control of stock thieves. It provided for a Board of Livestock Commissioners, who named *Inspectors* with power to arrest without warrant, conduct search-and-seizure, and in cases of extreme emergency to dispense justice under the articles of war. I say "passed." It had been voted down, actually, by the mining interests who controlled our legislature, who didn't want to be taxed, but later passed *in interim* with no funding. Those miners didn't have a care what happened on the plains as long as it didn't cost them anything. So with this doubtful authority the cattle interests went ahead.

A Board of Livestock Commissioners was duly named. Brig. General McKibbin was on it, representing our region. Two inspectors were appointed.

The act called for six, but two was all they had funds for. One of these was Ed Wiggin, whom we already met. The other was a cold and despicable killer named Jack Bushfield. As deputy U.S. Marshal in the Yellowstone Valley he hunted men down like wild animals, killed without hesitation or compunction, loading their warm bodies in gunny sacks which he bore back by packhorse. It was particularly horrible for those with dear friends and loved ones because they would stiffen with knees under chin, and some actually had to be placed in barrels for burial. I never seen it myself, but Rusty told about it, and Preacher Harlow averred it was true:

"It is indeed woeful to be up there to preach a funeral and have the body rolled in in a barrel," he said.

At any rate, that's what we were up against, and what the sheriff was up against. As long as he stuck with the posse he could exercise some control, but what if it was taken over by the likes of Bushfield? They'd declare emergency and hang Rusty perfectly legal. I wanted him to hustle in and give himself up.

The first place I went was our secret cabin. A message was stuck between the logs; it proved to be from Grace. I never snoop, as has already been made clear, but this I *had* to read in case there was a clue. "My dear, sweet, darling man," it said, and "Oh, Russell, I love you so," and she said how the roses were blooming, and she never smelled them but she remembered their first ride, etc., and a lot of very private stuff I skipped over. It made me go all soft and unsteady inside; it wasn't pleasant at all. I put it back, and looked for fresh sign. There wasn't any, only the tracks of some horses unshod, that had run wild from the range, and I cut over to Rocky Point on the river, reaching it one day later.

A steamboat was there, and left shortly after; it was a St. Louis boat, the New Era, very sleek and powerful, a far cry from the floating rafts you see plying out of Mandan, Dakota; Mr. Flanders, the trader, had me witness the condition of some goods delivered that had been damaged by rain; he had seen nothing of Rusty but promised to give my message to him; I wrote a short one and sealed it in an envelope, the first letter I ever wrote; and I headed back again, by way of Whiterock Creek, the Castle road, Turkeytail Rock, Breed's station and the Little Flatwillow—rather roundabout but places where Rusty was known. Finally, empty of success, I headed home.

Ranch all quiet. House was closed. This was strange because even when it stormed, and the rain blew, Ma left the door open to freshen. Cowboys watched from behind the sheds. Chickens unfed, follered me. Nobody would feed them but Ma; Dad Marsh might toss them some potato peels but cowboys thought it beneath their dignity—wouldn't milk a cow, either. Your typical cowboy doesn't want to do anything he can't do on a horse.

"Ma?" opening the door on the closed-in air. A note was propped against the sugar bowl.

Gone to Town

No explanation. The rifle stood in its accustomed place. Yet she seldom left without it. Very strange. I went down to the cookhouse.

"She's been arrested!" Dad Marsh said, not without relish. "You want to know who arrested her? Monte Sallows! He came here in his buggy and hauled her away to jail."

"When?"

"You hadn't been gone a day when he came in his rig."

"Did he say why?"

Of course nobody would tell Dad anything, but he had heard from somewhere that the order had been given by Lee Dougherty, the Association attorney. He claimed to have heard Monte say, "Thelma, I'm only an officer of the court."

None of the others knew a thing either, and they were just lying around, not doing a tap of work. They hadn't even kept the Enterprise cattle drive off our range. They didn't want to do it when I told them to, either. If I suggested the slightest thing they would sulk and resent it.

"We ain't been paid," said Ardis.

"You'll have to wait. Ma will probably bring back money from town." Though what they planned to spend it on I couldn't guess.

Headed for town. Fort Steele, a day's ride, set out on God's lonely prairie and one might well wonder why? Here's the fact: the Army had instructions to build in a place suitable to protect the road from the upper river ports to the gold fields. Fine and dandy, but the ports changed every year depending on how far the boats could travel up the river. Secondly, the gold fields moved year by year, depending on the new discoveries. Add to that the problem of building materials. We had no timber except cottonwood, which can't be sawed, so the answer had to be brick. The site for Steele was picked (a) because of a seam of red fluxing clay for brick, and (b) a good, shallow well water. Contracts were let, and up went a two-story headquarters, barracks, officers ball room, armory, you name it; then who should arrive but General of the Army William Tecumseh Sherman, and he rode through the worst autumn blizzard that had ever been seen. Oh! that was the finish of that. Work was stopped forthwith. He ordered a move to Fort Keogh, later Miles City, on the Yellowstone. Gold roads forgotten, he said the post was needed against the Indians. Typical Army thinking, Pa said, they posted themselves against the friendly Crows instead of the warlike Blackfeet,

Anyhow, Steele after languishing, prospered with the arrival of the cattle business. At the time of my visit it had grown to more than five hundred souls, or approximately ten per cent of all the white people in the eastern half of the territory. Business was booming. It was the height of the river season. The river was twenty miles away, at the closest, but Steele was much easier to get to. The goods were hauled there, handy for the customer. You could actually buy cheaper than you could at either the river ports, or down on the railroad. It was a question of volume, and competition. Ranchers came from as far off as the Judith and at that time were loading on October credit, when the beef money came.

I feared they might have a warrant out for me, but no one paid me the slightest heed. There was a fountain in front of the courthouse where you could water your horse. The courthouse, once the Army headquarters, was two-story, brick, very grand. Back of that was a lower addition, which served as a jail.

I watered, taking my sweet time, went inside. Government buildings always have a certain smell. All was empty of life. Much varnished wood, oak chairs, settees, hat trees, brass spittoons, a sign saying JUDGE. We had no resident judge. All the judges (federal) lived in the western third of the territory. Our Judge Van Orem traveled over from Benton. Tick-tock, tick-tock I could hear a clock, it was so quiet. I walked down a hall till the smell of jail assailed me. You always know first whiff.

"Oh, hello!" says Monte Sallows. "What are you doing?"

"Looking for Ma."

"She's not *here!*"

"I thought you arrested her."

"We're detaining her. She's at the hotel."

This meant the Wolverine Hotel. Terrible name, considering the nature of that animal, but logical enough seeing that the owners, Pat and Queenie Gilman, came from Michigan, "the wolverine state."

"What does 'detaining her' mean?"

I could see I had him uncomfortable. "You wouldn't understand it."

"Try me out!" I says, my heart beating like a hammer. "You mean she can come and go?"

"Well, yes. She's free to come and go as she likes here in town."

Sallows took me into his office. It was a little place without even a window.

"Have a drink?" he asked, setting out a bottle of whisky. Then he took it back. "You're not old enough."

"Yes, I am old enough!"

I took a swig right there. It was my second time only with whisky, aside from the medicine slings Ma made for me when I had a cold. I had a big one and it didn't even faze me, which showed how wrought up I was. Monte had one himself, with a great deal of water chaser, on account of his bad stomach.

"Any word about Rusty?" he asked.

"Nope."

"Did you look for him?"

"Yes, I did! I rode all the way to Rocky Point.

I could see he thought I was hiding Rusty's secret, whatever it happened to be. He should have known better. Rusty took nobody into his secrets; he was a free soul.

"Your mother will be very sorry to hear that you failed. I want you to look at this."

It was a telegram saying court was to convene at such and such an inst. and it was signed J.S. Darling, Clerk.

"I hope your brother doesn't make your mother bear the full weight of this matter."

"How about Crowfoot and Butler? They're the ones that drove the cattle." According to law "driving off customary range" was the essence, just as was "branding or altering brands of previously branded cattle." Nobody had seen anyone altering anything, all they had was circumstantial evidence, but we were eye witness that those steers had been driven off the *customary range!*

However this fell on deaf ears. "Their testimony wouldn't mean a thing. Nobody would believe either, given their reputation. Russell will have to be here to clear this matter up. You got to look at it from the owners' point of view." And he said something about the court being to our benefit. "They won't sit by. If we don't do something here in court they'll take the law into their own hands."

"They going to charge Ma?"

"That's why Rusty has to come in."

What was the use of talking? They were holding Ma for the single purpose of forcing Rusty to give himself up.

"Need any money for your keep?" asked the sheriff.

"Nope, I'll manage."

I left but didn't go straight to Ma. I went instead to find Rusty's lawyer, Vost Funderhide. He was down at the Buffalo Horn as usual, standing at the end of the bar with a newspaper spread out. He reminded you of a sandhill crane in build and posture. He wore a swaller tail coat even in the hottest weather, but left off his collar, and the shirt band was open with collar-button attached, and he had the biggest Adam's apple you ever saw. He had come from Kansas where he had got in trouble for making representations to save farmer lands from the railroad, and been disbarred. Many railroads were skin games organized for the single purpose of claiming lands under the law of eminent domain, but fortunately there are men like Funderhide willing to go to the wall for the dispossessed. He never applied for admittance to our bar, but acted through the firm of Kramer & McCabe, Miles City. We have so few lawyers they let him do everything except plead before the Montana Supreme court.

"Irons?" he says, fixing me with his gaze. "What word of your brother?"

"None."

"You'd better go get him."

He sounded just like Sallows. "What do you mean get him? They got him framed six ways from Sunday."

"All the more reason."

"I can't see that!"

"My dear boy, these people can do exactly as they please only as long as he stays away. Once he delivers up his corpus they'll have to decide on a specific charge. I can force their hands by calling for a grand jury, and they wouldn't like that."

"How come that hasn't been done for Ma?"

"For who?"

94

"Ma, my mother. She's being held without charge."

He took me into a back room and closed the door. "Rusty drove those steers to the ranch, didn't he?"

"No, he did not!"

"I happen to know he did."

"Well, you happen to know wrong."

"Never lie to your attorney."

"I ain't! Whose side are you on, anyhow?"

"I'm on your side. Those fellows wouldn't have had the brains to alter that Dakota registry.

"But Rusty would!"

"It goes without saying. The brand was on his chart in his office."

We went at it hot and heavy for a time, but he wasn't so angry as he seemed—it was just lawyer's talk—and when I said Crow Foot and Butler would lie for anybody that hired them he said, fine, and rubbed his dry hands, like talons, and said, "Fine! I'd ask for nothing better than a perjured witness. This Crow Foot is a jockey, and jockeys are always in bad repute." Then he shoves a paper at me and says, "Have you read this?"

CATTLE QUEEN
JAILED IN
FORT STEELE

It was in the Miles City paper, and they certainly had wasted no time. The *Stockman* had a similar item, and implied things very unfriendly considering we were pioneers. The local paper was fairest, carrying the bare-bones account, Ma being "questioned," about "allegations of improper impoundment," and in the Ye Editor Sez column, he asked whether

> in requiring these pioneer stock
> growers to hew the letter of the
> law we may be driving them the
> way of the buffalo?

It was the least he could do considering the amount Rusty spent on advertising. Every animal offered for sale required three insertions at the legal rate, and the brands had to be carved into what was called a blank em, which took the printer about two minutes and for which they charged a dollar extra, showing how the costs mount up when you set out to run a completely legal estray business.

The Billings paper had a lot about "the notorious Rusty Irons," and others had similar things, you never can know how fast news travels until it's bad news, and will *hurt* somebody. Funderhide subscribed to papers from near and far, keeping watch for deaths, relinquishments, suits to quiet title, etc., seeking to represent somebody for a percentage.

"These papers should be called to account!" I said.

"No, no. This is fine. This will bring him in if anything can. Have you talked with your mother?"

"Nope."

"Do so, and soon. I dare say she saw you ride in. Tell her our Judge Van Orem will arrive shortly. He conducts court now in Diamond City, and our turn will be next. For good or ill, her travail is nearly over." Laying a hand on my shoulder, "Be kind to your mother, boy. Never add to her gray hairs of trouble."

It was very decent attitude, considering what *she* thought of *him.*

"Oh, there you are!" says Ma. "You took your own sweet time!"

Mrs. Mooschbacker, a religious fanatic not of our faith was there, and we had to wait for her to gather up her tracts and vamoose.

"Well! Did you find Russell?"

"Nope. No word of him, anywhere."

"Oh, he's gone. He got us into this terrible trouble and went on another of his trips and abandoned us." So much for the tears. She got back to me and says, "Where'd you go? I can smell liquor on your breath."

"Had a drink from the sheriff," not without swagger.

"You are lying! He would not give whisky to a mere boy." I weighed near 160 pounds, more by five than Rusty, but I was still a child to her, big and shambling, "still at the awkward age;" then she says, "Monte Sallows did *not* give you drink, you got it down at the Buffalo Horn."

"No, I went there only to see Rusty's lawyer, Mr. Funderhide."

"Funderhide a lawyer? Why, he's a scalawag. He was drummed out by the profession!"

"He's associated with Kramer & McCabe of Miles City. He can appear before the Supreme Bench in a co-adjutor capacity."

"Oh, stop that big talk. What kind of a lawyer practices out of a saloon? And that *is* where you got your whisky, not from Monte Sallows!"

I let her have it her way. I let her talk at me as long as she liked to get it off her chest. We ate at the hotel, American plan. It appears that the Sheriff had vouched for us and hence we were entitled to all we could stuff into ourselves without it costing one thin dime. They served chicken and dumplings, early blister field corn, butter, and pie for dessert. I could have had a bed, too, but I decided to sleep where I put up my horse. It was a feed stable where you slept as part of the rate.

"No, I paid for it and I vow to use it!" I said, appealing to Ma's business sense. "Also, I might hear about Rusty. You get wind of everything at a feed stable."

True, but I heard nothing of Rusty. Then, one afternoon, just about when Judge Van Orem and his "legal circus" was due, the Helena coach rolled in, loaded to the rails, and there he was! The sheriff and Funderhide were both there to greet him. They had been informed.

"You are under arrest!" says Sallows, loud and clear.

"I surrender to your authority," responded Rusty.

And whilst the curious watched, those trine marched off the jail.

Chapter Nine

"I fear you will drink a bitter browst of your own brewing one day."

—*Quentin Durward*

Once they had Rusty locked up Ma was free to go home.

"No more riding the grubline for you, Thelma," says Monte Sallows with a big ha-ha. "The county will no longer pay your board and keep."

She wanted to visit him in the jail, but they wouldn't let her. They offered to bring him around to the hotel, but Rusty wouldn't stir.

"Oh, dear, what am I to do?" she said. "Blessed Savior, what is happening to our family? He is the first ever to be behind the bars."

Every day I went to see him and they let me walk right in. He might be lying in his cell, on his back, reading and smoking, or he might be playing cribbage with Fossbender, or one of the deputies, who liked to loaf in the jail, where it was cool. It was a real good jail, built as I pointed out, by the Army, who did things right, all solid brick, double walled, and not a log chicken coop as in so many of your Western towns.

Rusty was a good card player; he would talk all the time, and make people laugh, but his brain was working on another level, and he'd take your money away from you before you knew what happened, but he let the deputies win a little to keep them happy.

The judge and his retinue arrived. They had a three-seater surrey and a supply wagon. The supply wagon seemed to be full of books. Six men rode in the surrey, plus the driver, and two more in the supply wagon. Several came by stage. Most of them were lawyers. "The locusts," people called them. They called themselves the same, thinking it funny. They put up at the Wolverine and at the Majestic, the latter being a hotel and also a house of ill repute; but Judge Van Orem himself was put up at the home of T.R. Gibbons, merchant and steamboat owner. Both were up high in the Masonic Lodge, 32nd degree, Gibbons being Grand Worshipful Master while Van Orem had been Grand Loyal Keeper of the Ninth Arch of the Al Haddad Shrine in Virginia City. This was *our* Virginia City, not the one in Nevada. The Masons were very strong in Montana Territory and comprised the heart and soul of the vigilante committees, as could be guessed from the disproportionate number of Irish Catholics hung. So Rusty said. There was a soirée at Gibbons' that night, and from the hotel porch you could hear music over the sing of mosquitoes. Next morning the gavel fell . . .

The first thing they did was find a real good place for Ma to sit, not as a prisoner, but more of an honored guest. "As befitting one of our true pioneers!" says Van Orem, making a little speech. This meant I got a prime chair as well.

They went through papers for a long time, the Judge and his secretary, and every so often Lee Dougherty would get up and preen himself. He acted next unto God with his Roman bearing, and his hair cut in noble featheredge. His friend and cronies called him "Senator" because he had been mentioned for that office when and if Montana attained statehood. All the chairs taken, people stood in the back, and out in the hall where smoking was allowed. At last Van Oren said something, the clerk went out, and pretty soon in came Monte Sallows with Rusty. There was a great gawking to see what he looked like; you'd think he'd be known by everyone in the land but people arrived every year by sheer hundreds. That was part of our trouble, too many cattle and too many people.

Rusty didn't look at Ma. He sat down with Funderhide at a small table.

"Mr. Russell T. Irons?" says Van Orem.

"Yes," standing.

He wrote something down.

"You may sit."

Rusty sat.

"Your Honor, I have an information for the court," says Lee Dougherty.

"Objection," says Funderhide.

"For what reason?" says Van Orem, surprised.

"Federal Attorney is also attorney for the Buffalo Lakes Roundup Association, one of the complainants."

"No such complaint in hand," says the Judge.

However, Funderhide stayed on his pins and went into a long harangue about how a true bill was called for, an indictment only after the matter was presented to a full grand jury of his peers, etc.

"Mr. Dougherty, what say you to this?" asked Van Orem.

Dougherty rose, rugged and self-possessed, smiling to show that the likes of Funderhide were not to be taken seriously, but should be allowed to rant for a while, it didn't do any harm.

"We meet here in the full blaze of day!" he says, striking a posture. He was certainly a handsome man. Like him or no, you had to admit it. He had a real moose of a nose, and his gray-shot hair flowed back in careful disarray. "I look around me and see that evidence of democratic justice which makes America great. This might in old New England be regarded as a town meeting. Peers, you say? We are all peers! I heard mention made of a grand jury. But does this not in fact constitute that very thing, except on a more democratic scale?"

"But do we meet our accusors face to face?" cut in Funderhide.

Dougherty waved a hand indicating well, we shouldn't worry too much about *that*. No shortage of accusers in *this* case, ha-ha. He didn't actually say it, though. He didn't *say* anything he didn't want on the record. As he talked he walked over from time to time to see what was written down. The clerk wrote steadily even during times of quiet, catching up, I suppose. He must have had to carry it in his head. There follered a lot of argument about sworn statements and depositions, and they got to shuffling through some documents and discussing their nature low-voiced, clerk's pen at rest.

"How about this man, is he an Indian?" asked Orem.

"No, nickname."

"That's an alias," said Funderhide.

"It's a sobriquet, a nom-de-terre."

They were arguing about Crowfoot.

"But how is he signed here?" asked Van Orem.

"Lynwood Peabody. 'The Crow Foot Kid.' "

"Peabody!" cried Funderhide. "Is he of the Boston Peabodys?" he asked, which really was funny if you happened to know Crowfoot and what a no-good little squirt he was.

"Your honor!" cried Dougherty, back on the record, "it was not the prosecution which chose to introduce the name of Peabody, or Crow's Foot, or whatever, into this matter." And he set forth this and that, and the "contention of Mrs. Irons," and whether said parties had been at the Irons house on this or that date, that said parties recalled no such journey, no such delivery, and had so deposed.

"Depose? Deposition?" cried Funderhide. "That is not best evidence. These men must be produced in person!"

So it went, on and on, and I was too mixed up to understand what they were out to prove. There was a lot of talk about the meaning of estray, and customary range, and whether presence of livestock in an enclosed pasture was proof of possession, or whether sale was paramount, and then Funderhide said he would like to speak with his client, and the judge said he would recess for fifteen minutes.

Few left for fear of losing their seats, but Rusty and Funderhide stood by a window and talked, and the Judge and Dougherty and several more repaired to an inner chamber to smoke and talk about duck hunting. I couldn't hear them, but I could see them swinging imaginary shotguns around. They had something to drink, too. I caught a strong whiff of the old aged in the wood when they returned. *Bang!* goes the hammer

"Mr. Funderhide?"

It was not our turn.

"Your honor, what have we here truly?" he says.

103

"Six cattle on a fenced pasture. Distinguished attorney says, 'Out of public view.' Why, goodness gracious, said pasture is traversed by a public road, as marked on government map." Then he told how Ma had accepted the cattle in good faith from two men who averred them to be estrayed from far-off Dakota. "Now, it is not my wish to put Mrs. Irons on the witness stand under oath"—he bowed to her—"a pioneer woman, universally respected, nor her young son"—motioning at me—"for inasmuch as the Association attorney has not seen fit to produce witnesses, but asks the court to rely on depositions, or second-best evidence, and it not being our wish to cost the territory, and this hard-pressed court, more time and money, why . . ."

He knew everybody was watching, wondering what he was about to do, and he went over and got an old leather portfolio, which he unbuckled. There seemed to be only a single item inside. It was a paper, or letter. By the looks it had been carried in pocket for many a mile: when it was opened you could see dirt and wear at the folds. He struck a posture and showed it this way and that to one and all. As far as Funderhide was concerned the spectators were the important thing, not the court. Finally he fixed some glasses on his nose, and he cleared his throat.

"Receipt!"

You could see the word RECEIPT printed in big letters across the top. It looked as if it had been lettered in bullet lead. I don't suppose there was a soul there that hadn't used a bullet instead of a pencil in emergency. In fact, many a claim notice was written out in bullet rather than pencil as a warning.

" 'Received of Russell Irons the sum of forty dollars,' parenthesis, 'gold coin, as finder's fee in full for eight heavy red steers, longhorn crossbreed, branded Snake S on left sides. Undersigned do hereby attest all were found estray as term is defined by Montana Territorial Statutes, same being delivered this day, June 12,' signed, 'T.S. Soles,' and signed also, 'Benjamin,' that is B-E-N-J, period, 'Benjamin Butler.' "

Well, out of his chair came Dougherty. "Let me see that!" he cried, trying to snatch it away.

"My pleasure," but he laid it in front of the clerk.

"These are not genuine signatures!"

"How does attorney know?"

"By simple comparison."

"True," says Funderhide, smug as could be, "*one* of them has to be a forgery. The question is which one."

Dougherty still couldn't get his hands on the paper. The clerk passed it on to Van Orem.

"Who is this 'T.S. Soles?'"

"T.S. Soles and not 'Peabody' is the true name of the Crow Foot Kid!"

"Is this written in bullet lead?"

"Forty-four calibre!" says Rusty.

"Do you wish your client to so testify? If so he will be placed under oath."

"No, I would ask the remark be stricken."

"Objection!" said Dougherty.

"It's not part of the record anyway," said Van Orem. "Is it?" he asked the clerk, who shook his head.

I couldn't figure out what was going on. They got to talking about some race over in Fort Benton where Crowfoot had ridden McFadden's black mare and some other party had lost a bundle of money. People even got to calling things from the audience. It truly galled Ma they would act that way when a person's liberty was at stake.

"It's just a hearing," I told her.

At last they got back to the business at hand and the sheriff was asked how long it would take for him to produce the witness in question, and the sheriff said "a week or two, maybe more," and Van Orem said, "Information accepted. Indictment in due course. Party bound over to next term of court."

"Hold on!" cried Funderhide. "With what is my client charged?"

"Why, removal of cattle from customary range."

"No," said Dougherty, "grand larceny."

"Oh yes, I was reading the particulars."

"Your honor, can't those be reserved? The matter is still under investigation."

"How does your client plead, guilty or not guilty?"

"I want to read the information."

"Plea of not guilty accepted. Is that all right with you? You don't want to plead guilty, do you?"

"No!" says Rusty.

"Pleads not guilty."

"Will court set bail?"

"Objection!" cried Dougherty. "We ask that bail be denied."

"For what reason?"

"By reason of this man's wandering habits. The territory does not hold him."

They jawed about it for a while, and the Judge and secretary held a whispered conversation, and then Van Orem said, "Motion denied."

At least we'd come up with something. Like so many other judges and attorneys Van Orem had his eye on political office. He thirsted for the governorship, and, barring that, the post of Territorial Secretary, and thinks I in my innocence he didn't want to get people down on him by the appearance of knuckling under to powers such as Dougherty, McKibbin, Hoffner, etc. But was I to be disabused!

"Bail granted."

"In what amount?" asked Funderhide.

"In the amount," he whispered for a time with Dougherty, "in the amount of ten thousand dollars."

Well, people just sat there. They couldn't believe he'd said it. Nobody had heard of such a bail. A thousand dollars bond was considered average. Of course all our prices were high, a hat cost you half again to twice as much in Steele as it did in St. Paul. But ten thousand dollars was a fortune! You could take ten thousand and move right on easy street and never have to do another tap of work as long as you lived. The Judge made $4,000 yearly but that included his honorariums from private practice. Cavalrymen made $13 per month was why they were overjoyed to get out and take jobs as cowboys ($20) even though they had to buy their own clothes and gear. So ten thousand dollars!

Well, by the time they got over their surprise he had banged his gavel and said court was adjourned until two o'clock when Budlow vs. the United States would be called, that or some similar land case, and he stood up.

"Will the court reconsider?" Funderhide said. "Your honor!" etc., but did he duck out in a hurry!

I think Rusty was the coolest one of the lot. He just sat there with a little smile. Thought for a while he was going to roll a cigarette, but he didn't. The next coolest one, I'd say, was Dougherty, and their eyes met. It had all been arranged between the attorney and the judge, they knew exactly what was to be done, and they'd done it! "You blankety-blank, son of a b- - -h!" Rusty seemed to say. "You really did it to me!"

Chapter Ten

Come open your gates, and let me gae free
I durna stay longer in bonny Dundee.
—Rob Roy

Ma was willing to sign the ten thousand dollar bond, farfetched as it may seem, but Rusty wouldn't let her do it.

"It would be the last anybody ever saw of me."

"You mean you'd skip bail? I don't believe it!"

"I'd fail to appear. They'd make sure of that!"

"He means, little mother, he'd take residence 'in that land from whose bourne no traveler returns,' " said Funderhide.

"They'd deep-gulch me, Ma, and they'd cave the bank over me, and none but the wandering wolf would know the spot."

"Oh, I don't believe it!"

I says, "Look what happened to Pa!"

"You be quiet! If they'd wanted to shoot you they'd have done so long ago."

Ma sure seemed thick-headed at times. She couldn't see that they'd shoot him, and never breathe a word, and the bail would be forfeit, and they'd have won it all—got rid of Rusty, and us, too. The court could seize our land, water right, range, everything. They'd divide us up.

"Oh, dear! I can't leave you behind bars."

"You can and will. Hank, get her out of here. Take her back to the ranch. Make her stay at the ranch. And don't sign anything!"

"I'm not going! I'll not be known as a mother that abandons her children."

He turned to Fossbender the jailer, who stood key in hand. "Take her out, Foss. Look at it this way, Ma—for once you'll know where to find me."

She stood there, and stood there, but finally she let Funderhide and me lead her from the door.

"Has he got any money to hire lawyers?" she said. "Where's the money coming from?"

"Don't worry about that," says Funderhide, "Everything possible will be done. I'll lay the matter before the supreme court, if necessary."

"Oh, big talk!"

"Now-now, Mrs. Irons. Justice will be found."

"Go and get your clothes cleaned! You'll get no place in that reeking suit."

He laughed and said, "All right, Mrs. Irons. All right. We'll even see about a new suit. And I'll retain C.F. Chowndley as my associate in the matter." Chowndley was about the biggest lawyer in the territory, with the Northern Pacific Railroad as client.

"Oh, dear! That will cost us a fortune. Will the costs never cease?"

"Don't worry about that, little mother. Claude Chowndley owes me a couple of favors and it will not cost an additional red cent."

Big talk is right! But it gave her some comfort just the same.

I was obliged to rent a rig in order to get Ma home. The sheriff *should* have done it, but he didn't offer, and Ma wouldn't let me ask him.

"No, I don't want to be beholding!"

We got an early start, hence making it on a single day, and unlike traveling with Rusty, Ma had got them to put up a lunch for us at the hotel.

"Thank God, home at last!" says Ma with a mighty sigh, and went about chasing out the animals that always take over a house after long absence—mice, packrats, garter snakes and cottontail rabbits; these latter were in a sense welcome because it meant no skunks; skunks rush in to occupy under a floor as soon as humans depart, and sometimes before, but when they do certain animals depart, and among these are rabbits. Rabbits are not overly fond of rattlesnakes, either, but packrats move right in with them as cozy as you please.

So much for that. She cleaned up what the animals had strewn around, put them in their place as it were, and the men all got down to work, and Preacher Harlow and Lucius Engate came poking around, they had been watching the ranch for Rusty.

"They got him in jail," I told them. "Under ten thousand dollars bond." You'd think he'd scored some overweening success by how they acted, you'd think he was a regular Jesse H. James in the flesh.

"Ten thousand dollars bond!" yells the Preacher. "That's Rusty! He was always a top hand!"

Ma didn't welcome them, so they pulled out after a day, driving some saddle stock of the Rocking Chair brand, for which they had the papers. When things were going along as well as usual, and all the men were at work, I set out to return the team and buggy.

"What are *you* doing here?" asked Rusty when they let me in.

There he lay, hat on as usual. It was suppertime and

the floor nearby was littered with plates and the remains of T-bone steak, fried potato, pie, etc. He seemed to be living pretty high for a prisoner. A restaurant fed the prisoners for 50¢ per day, but you could order meals sent in if you had the money.

"Hungry?"

"I'll make out."

"How are things at the ranch?"

"Same."

"Any mail?"

"Nothing much. Magazines, papers."

"When you going back?"

"That depends. I wanted to talk to you."

"You are talking to me. I want you to leave."

"Right now?"

"Yes, get out, shake the dust, vamoose."

I must have looked at him with the shock I felt because he sat up, put his feet on the floor, and gave me about as hard a look as I'd ever received.

"I don't want you around here. I don't want you around town! You shouldn't leave Ma out there by herself. You're the man of that spread, and you'll have to take responsibility."

"Ma wanted me to pick up some stuff."

"Pick it up and go!"

"I wouldn't get farther than Fraley's before dark, anyhow. I'd be stuck out there on that lonesome bench all night."

"Where are you now?"

"Huh? Why, right here."

"Where'd you put up?"

"Oh. Well, I left my horse at the feed stable."

"Tom Bedloe?"

"Yes. He lent us the rig. He wouldn't take a cent."

"Why not?"

112

"He said he'd bill the county and if they didn't pay we could settle later."

"You figure on bedding down there?" He was reconsidering.

"Yes."

"Don't do it. If you're going to stay, make it the hotel. See if you can share a room with somebody. A drummer or something."

I couldn't figure whether he was joking or not.

"Do what I tell you to! Money don't grow on trees!"

"All right."

"Stay right there and have breakfast. Here's two dollars. Now, I don't want you to stir from that hotel between ten o'clock tonight and breakfast tomorrow!"

I knew it was no use to ask. He wasn't going to tell me a thing.

"I want to end up the year with at least one of the Irons boys alive!" This was for the benefit of any who were listening. "That d- - -Hoffner!" as if he was the chief one to be afraid of. (But this wasn't true at all. Brigadier McKibbin was the true culprit. The voice might be the voice of Jacob, but the hand was the hand of Esau!)

I accepted Rusty's two dollars, it was easier than to argue, but I didn't go near the hotel; I had supper at the Chinese restaurant—roast pork with dressing and gravy, green peas and new potatoes, and maple cake —60¢ but worth it!—and retired along with my saddle horse, which had been there since what seemed eons ago, or out in pasture.

I could hear him in the nearby stall, and myself picked a place in the hay. This was old hay, horses won't eat hay that's been slept in, not unless they're starving, and was the customary place for people to sleep. You bed down after dark, and then move, if you like; i.e. if you're worried about being robbed or stabbed in the night. It happens rarely, but it *does* happen, and there's no harm playing safe. I said *stabbed* because shooting in a barn is a real capital crime, on account of fire, and you'd have to answer to the public. Smoking after dark also puts you absolutely beyond the pale, also. You are ten times more likely to be shot in a hotel as a barn, this is an established fact.

"Irons!"

I thought I was dreaming. I thought I was lying with my face in a fire and somebody was rousing me on that account. I sat up and saw the fire was the sun, it was beaming hot through an open end of the shed right into my face.

"Irons!" I woke up to a braying voice and people storming through the hay. Thought the barn was on fire, having been thinking about fire the previous night, but it was the sun, shining through the posts.

I had a pistol in reach, under the hay, but I left it there. You can bet I did, because the voice belonged to Casey Hobbs, the deputy, a very brutal customer. Everybody said so, and wondered that Sallows kept him on. He'd walk up to arrest a man and just knock him down with his pistol.

"Come out of there!" brays Casey Hobbs, the bully. "Get a move on!" He actually kicked me when I tried to scramble. "Where's your gun?"

"I ain't got a gun."

He practically said I was a liar, no whelp would lie to him, etc., and "Where's your brother?"

"I don't know. Ain't he in jail?"

"You know he's not in jail!"

My spirits leaped despite all.

"Last I saw he was in jail." But they weren't listening. I asked what had happened? No answer to this civil question. The sheriff then came in with Bedloe, the owner.

"Where'd you get this Diamond R horse?" Hobbs yelled at me.

"It's our horse! I rode him in, how'd you think he got here?"

"Oh, don't be a fool," says Monte Sallows. "How many horses did the Irons' board here the last week?" he asked Bedloe.

They talked about the team I'd brought back, and the sheriff looked at them. Then he got me to one side and said, "This is a very bad situation. You could go to prison."

"For what? Nobody's told me a thing."

They didn't then, either. I started to gather my things, but Hobbs gave me such a shove I almost fell down. The sheriff saw it but ignored it. He wanted to show that being a family friend meant no difference in my treatment. I went as bid and every time I slacked in the slightest, even when somebody got in front, Casey Hobbs would give me another shove. We headed across town.

There was a quite a crowd at the courthouse. We went in by the side door. Hobbs led me into Sallows' office.

"Now, listen to me!" he says. "I hate to see a young fellow get himself into trouble. But you'll be in up to your nose if you don't make a clean breast of it."

"Of what? I don't even know what happened."

"You came in here yesterday and passed something to your brother and we want to know what it was."

"I did no such thing. I just talked to him."

x

115

I expected to get knocked flat, but he never made a move.

"I want to know what you told him. Was it a message?"

"I told him what was happening at the ranch."

"You just left town. What were you doing back again?"

"I had to return the team and buggy. Monte Sallows came out and arrested Ma, and he never took her back! Like he should have." It was a risk, but I said it. However, his mind seemed to be on other things.

All of a sudden he says, "Where's Preacher Harlow?"

"I don't know!"

"You saw Lucius Engate, I know that."

"Who?"

He meant The Ringbone Kid. We never called him other. He kept shooting questions about one or another of Rusty's friends, but to no avail, and finally he walked out and left me. The door was open, nobody came, so I moseyed along to where the excitement was, in the jail. There were two cells and a big room with a table, and another room where the jailer slept. Eight or nine people were there. They didn't pay the slightest attention to me. The jailer, a deputy named Fossbender, sat at a table, looking miserable. They were waiting for somebody, and he showed up—Lee Dougherty. He must have heard all about it because the first thing he did was shout at Fossbender,

"Where'd you go last night?"

"Not a damn place! I was right here!"

"You left and came back. You turned in before checking the cells."

"I did not. Vorgey came in about nine and we

116

played some two-handed pitch. Ask him. Smitty was here, too!"

"Where was Irons?"

This jolted me, but he meant Rusty, not me.

"He was right there in that cell!"

"Was he there, or out here playing cards?"

"No, he was in his cell! Ask them, ask anybody."

"Did you see him in there or did you just assume?" However, he went on to the next question, "Was the door locked?"

"No, but I locked it. I locked it, turned the key all the way, and tried it, hard, like I always do. I told him he'd have to put out his lamp. I don't allow reading after I lock up for the night."

"How about these other doors? Could somebody have walked in?"

"No, *they could not!* I barred the corridor and went to my room. You can ask Vorgey. He went out and I locked up. Then I went in to my room the same as always. All of my windows are *nailed shut.* He'd have had to clumb acrost my bed."

Foxy and sharp, Dougherty shot a question, "How much did you have to drink?" but Fossbender was not taken by surprise.

"Nothing! Not a drop!"

"Then you got up in the morning and he had just vanished?"

"Into the thin air!" cried Fossbender.

"What time was this?"

"About half past six."

"That your usual hour?"

"Yes, give or take—"

"You didn't notify the sheriff till after seven."

"That's true." He was truly uncomfortable. "I never

117

suspected he was gone. It's dark in there. And all was locked and shipshape."

"Oh, - - - -!" He said a vile word, the very epitome of disgust. "You left the keys where he could reach them."

Fossbender kept on denying; he swore up and down that he had hung the keys above his bed, and they were still there, exactly the way he had hung them, etc. "Anyhow, even if he had got hold of them there's absolutely no way they can be fitted from inside."

You had to believe he was either telling the truth or believed he was telling the truth, because he was truly in a *state*, grey faced, gaunt and atremble.

"How many sets of keys are there?"

"Just mine. I got the only ones."

"No, there's a set over in the bank vault," somebody said. Wally Bell, one of the part-time deputies was sent over to check, and they were there, undisturbed.

"This has happened before," said Lee Dougherty.

"Not by me, it didn't. I had nothing to do with that."

His wife, much younger, had lived with him in the jail and cooked for the prisoners; they got 50 cents per head for this and had a pretty good thing, but about a year and a half before she had run off with a forger, who was serving a term of ninety days. He had served about 85 of them when they lit out. Nothing was done.

Lee kept looking at me, and looking, and finally said, "Hey, aren't you the Irons boy?"

"Yup," says I.

"What are you doing here?"

I wasn't doing much of anything, just standing around, I'd been brought there, and the sheriff said there was no way I could have been involved, I had come in to return a livery rig, and had been asleep at the barn, Bedloe had verified it, etc., but Dougherty was in no mood to listen.

"I suppose you'll go to him and make a report! By God, this takes the cake!" He laughed, but oh! how bitter. "I'd understood that Gaul was divided into three parts, but you got it all! Son, I'd like to shake you by the hand!" And he did, for quite a while, with firm clasp, but I was distinctly uncomfortable. "Wait a second! Here's a dollar. This sort of a thing ought to be rewarded!"

I wouldn't take the dollar, however, and I slipped away and got saddled and lit out as soon as decently possible.

Chapter Eleven

". . . . Ride your ways, Laird of Ellangowan—ride your ways, Godfrey Bertram—This day ye quenched eleven smoking hearths—see if the fire in your ain parlour burn the blither for that!"
                                        —Guy Mannering

H ome again. We had to pay our men, though little work did they do. They could have earned considerably more from one of the big outfits, as much as $40 per month, but more likely to be cut adrift after beef roundup. We kept them on all year. Ma tried to borrow the money in Steele and was turned down flat.

"Why, we never been refused before."

"So I see," says the new cashier, smooth and nasty. "We have this note unpaid since last fall."

"It's secured by beef on the range."

"We would have to have additional certification."

He meant it would have to be verified by the Association. She's have to go to Dougherty.

"How will I pay my men? What good are banks if they can't tide over their customers in a time of need?"

But it did no good. Under his black silk vest lay a heart of stone.

We did get credit for groceries and left town with a

buggyload, including half a case of cartridges for the old Sharps. This didn't mean we were loading for war, only that .50 calibres weren't always kept in stock.

"Are the buffalo coming back, Mrs. Irons?"

"I wish they was!"

Clippety-clop, clippety-clop went the hoofs for mile on mile and hardly a word, because Ma was troubled. She would just stare across the land, and then she might startle you with something like, "Oh, Pa! Send us some sign. Tell me what to do." Or she would plead for his understanding: "Pa, I'm holding on as best I'm able, but it's hard, hard. I'm near the end of my rope." It was eerie, I'll tell you! I kept getting the sense of somebody watching, but there was nothing but emptiness, land and sky.

Ma was a very religious woman, also devoted to spiritualism. There was a psychic medium in Fort Benton, a woman by the name of Hettie Folz, who claimed to have contacted Pa's spirit, though little of import came through. She said reaching the nether world was an arduous process, as the road was unknown and had many turnings. Ma visited her twice at $2 per call and kept a slate and steel ready to put down whatever came to her for later interpretation which was to be part of the deal. It was particularly important, Hettie Folz said, to put down things that came to you in the dream state after dark. Ma did so, but nothing could be made out except for *gno, elbic* and a lot of letters trailing off into squiggles. No matter, she was to stare at these until her eyes grew heavy and if any thoughts came she was to set them down. I truly hoped something might come of it, and Pa would tell us who had shot him, but Rusty laughed and made fun of the whole thing. He said Ma was throwing her money away; if that old crone in Benton could get messages from the Almighty why hadn't she turned some to her own account? She lived in a hovel and was breadcrust poor. Rusty said the fact was when you were dead you were dead, and a good thing, too, because you could just imagine what it would be like with all the ghosts whisking about, millions of them. I tended to agree, but just the same a number of occurrences could not be readily explained:

For instance, one morning we got up and found that a book had been taken down from a shelf in Pa's old office and opened to a certain page. Ma asked had I taken it down? I hadn't, and she hadn't, yet there it was! It was only a book on horse training he had got with a subscription, and there wasn't a thing we could see on the open page which seemed to have any "attribution," but Ma said it could be just the matter of finding "the key." Then one night I woke up to the most terrible stillness, a dense quality, so you could hardly breathe, and I heard something. It was a whispery sound, but it proved to be Ma, up prowling about.

"Pa?" she says. "Pa? Speak to me."

It chilled right to the bone, and I lay without breathing while this went on and on, and here is the strange part: you could tell by the time she just stood quiet that she was listening, and hearing something that was said, but for her ears alone. Next morning I hinted and waited for her to tell me about it, but she cut me off short saying, "You must have been *imagining*. I never do walk in my sleep."

Dad Marsh saw her up and around, and had heard her talking to him, and he himself claimed to have seen Pa *twice*, once walking by moonlight, and once in the afternoon when he woke up from his nap. The second one shook him the most. He said something caused him to wake earlier than usual, and there stood Pa as in life. He first thought the past year or two had been a dream, and Pa hadn't been shot. He was about to speak, but he noticed that Pa wasn't even looking at him, that is he was looking right past him as if he wasn't even there, or into another world, and then, slowly, he faded off. He didn't *drop* as ghosts are said to do.

Rusty said Dad Marsh was an old liar. They didn't get on at all. Dad wouldn't say boo to Rusty but he was after me all the time.

"Where's all that money your brother was supposed to have brought back from Deadwood?" he'd ask.

"I don't regard that as your affair."

Oh, was he mad! "Why, you slick-nut! Don't come around here with your sass or I'll give you acrost the head with a skillet!"

Then he'd tell about what a man of action he had been back in the olden days when him and Will came to the land. He had an old needlegun which some English hunter had brought to the country. You couldn't buy cartridges for it, but he had some he hoarded and shot off about one per year. To hear him talk you would think it the greatest firearm since the invention of steel. Also, if I tried to give an order it was resented. Not only by him but by the others. They'd smirk, and stall around, and not do it, and then if I went and complained to Ma they'd say I was a tattletale. So you see what I was up against.

They didn't come looking for Rusty, though I suspect the ranch was watched. I rode out and around looking for sign. Particularly I looked for the small boot tracks which would show that Grace had been there. Nothing. One time I found some spit-stained, dry cigarettes, but *they* weren't hers!

Tom Reedy, a rancher from Shoe Coulee, stopped on his way from town with news that there was a new sheriff. Monte Sallows had left for a course of treatments back east. He had departed for the Homeopathic Clinic in Orton, Maryland.

"Did he *resign?*" asked Ma.

"Not as I know, but he named Hobbs to be acting sheriff. The first thing Casey did was get rid of Smith. Put on Ed Peale, Long Henry Carmichael and Dalton Reeves."

"Why, they're no better than gunmen! They'll be the scourge of the land!"

Now in truth did I have to locate Rusty! Rode all the way to McKibbin's and watched the ranch for hours and hours. It looked like they had a batch of guests. Ever and anon there came guests to McKibbin's, from Helena, from the capital, from back East. I was certain I saw Grace, on horseback—I knew by how she rode, and wore her hat, held by a chin string, on the back of her head—but always were others along.

I slept in the open, with naught but saddle blanket, then returned home, kept watch of the roads from the Organ Pipes, our most prominent landmark; watched for Rusty with one eye and for Hobbs and his gang of deputies with the other, and at last set out for Goose Honker's on the outside chance I'd find him there.

All very still and quiet. Deer were around. Away they went, not too wild, with stiff little hops which showed they'd not been shot at, knew not the evil intent of man. Nobody was there, nor had been there in quite a while. No messages left.

It was so quiet and restful after the long, dry travel

that I was almost glad. It was truly fine, with the smells of evening rising. Picketed my horse well up the coulee and walked back. Didn't want to get took by surprise. Built a fire in the little sheet metal stove and made doughgod with bacon in the middle. Much time consumed in this but worth the waiting. Such doughgods are a trifle greasy, but very good. Have to eat them with the sleeves rolled up. Put out the fire, cleaned everything, completely. I'd have done this whether wary of human visitors or not. Animals without number catch the smell of food and pester you. Wolves, coyotes, even grizzly bears which you saw about once per year, and skunks which are worst of all. All the world is famished and only man deems it strange. With such thoughts I puttered around when a sound, or something like a sound, brought me up sharp.

I listened and listened. What I'd heard was not a sound in actuality, but a *memory* of sound, as of an echo which hangs and speaks forth a second time, or the music that hangs on a fiddle string long after the bow has been put aside. And of course it was the time of day, neither day nor night, or what is called "the crepuscular gloom" when the shadows form, and take on a life.

Then Rusty's voice came to me, also the click of a hoof, and I almost called out in greeting.

Caution stilled me. He was talking to somebody else. Still far-off, too. The ears as well as the eyes can trick you at that witching hour.

"Hey, Duke!"

That was the retriever that accompanied Grace. It meant she was along. I know this seems far-fetched, but I actually caught a whiff of her—her perfume, and the other smells that were *her*, a girl smell, and all the fresh air.

They were still distant. It was absolutely still, or seemed to be, but a breath of wind must have passed up the draw, bearing the smells from the distance. Like at night when you might smell the river from miles and miles off.

I had time to hustle around and remove the signs of my being there. Wasn't sure they'd be happy to find me. "Three's company," Ma often said, "but two starts a scandal." The fire was all cold, I'd already extinguished it, and as ere stated my horse was removed, so I faded into the gloom.

They arrived in due course, I could hear them down at the cabin, and pretty soon, as might be expected, the dog smelled me out.

"Woof!" he goes, but he knew me.

This left me in a quandary. I didn't want to take the chance of being found out, hiding and spying. I *wasn't* spying, but it might look like. So back I went.

"Woof! woof!" goes Duke, happy as could be, like he was saying "Look who I found!"

They must have been inside the house because Rusty said, "Get away from here!" and "Ki-yi!" from Duke as if he'd been kicked.

I explain all this so it will be understood that I was not a snooper or a sneak.

"Oh, Russell, *no!*" says Grace, and she wasn't talking about his kicking old Duke.

"Why not?" says he.

"You know why."

"Oh, it's all right. I'm sure it is." Then she said something and he said, "You can do it up to the seventh month."

I knew what they were about! It gave me the worst

feeling you can imagine. I couldn't walk, or scarcely stand, and it was as if my intestines might fall out. They were going to do what they'd done that night at the Association meeting, when he'd left me alone in the barn, and I'd known they'd done because of how he smelled when he came back. No wonder the Brigadier had strung him up and whipped him!

Understand, I don't excuse the Brigadier, what he'd done was terrible, but I do say it can be understood. I felt a little ill towards him myself, if you must know the truth. Jealousy enters in. We are all but human!

I could hear the jingle of her buckles when she took off her riding skirt, and I got a whiff of Rusty's feet when he took off his boots, even as I made hustle to get away from there, vanish, seek out the land of never was. Duke follered me for a while and separated at last. I rode off without saddling, bareback and carrying my saddle over my own back, and on for untold miles until I gave out, and dismounted, and rested with my back against a dirt bank, and slept, and morning dawned at last. Magpies woke me. My horse must have picked the spot because there was green feed, no water but the sort of low bush that indicated there was water not far beneath. Saddled and rode, found the prairie rim with distant landmarks, the events of the past evening like unto a dream . . .

Chapter Twelve

"Would ye ride into the maw o' the Deil?"
—Redgauntlet

"Where you been?" Ma asked me. "Out badlanding with your no-good brother?"

"Nope." Hadn't, actually, and at all events I'd have kept mum. Anyway, in about a week here he came, with a number of riders, Preacher, Ringbone, Artie Johnson, and a couple more I didn't know, driving three poor looking strays. "In broad daylight!" Ma expostulated.

Rusty pretended she was talking about the cattle, that he shouldn't be driving them, and Ma said, "You know what I mean! You broke jail."

"I broke nothing. I walked out."

"You escaped as defined by the law. You can be shot on sight."

"Ma, this is the United States, not Mexico. Mexico is where they have the *fuga-lay.*"

"They have a new sheriff and he's out to shoot you on sight. What gang is that you brought along?"

"Not a gang, they're old friends."

"They're badlanders, and they have illegal cattle."

"Those are estrays, and can be so certified."

"How?"

"By posting and advertising in the newspaper."

"In what newspaper? You don't dare show your face."

"I'll ride in there a free citizen and ride out the same way."

He meant it! He meant to ride in with his badlanders, Preacher, Ringbone, et al. He turns to me and says, "How about it, little brother? Would you like to go in to town?"

"You will *not* take that boy!" Ma said, and much more, but she gave in when I said I was set to go. I think she figured Rusty would do nothing outrageous with me in hand.

We didn't set out right away. He sat up half the night by candle doing something. After his jaunt with Grace he must have had some business to attend to down along the river, and he had been to T.S. Gregory's. Gregory was the true owner of those red steers.

"You want to know how I escaped from jail?" he asked out of a blue sky.

I said yes, I did, and he gave a long account of how he had secured some rawhide, and made a chunk of it, about half an inch by two, and he'd packed it into the lock of his cell door, into the arbor or slot, right where the bolt would come against it, just snug enough to hold back the bolt but not let the click fall, and how when Fossbender went to bed he rose from his cot and urinated on it, it was just the right height for him to do that, and he repeated with a squirt now and again, and the rawhide, as it will, swelled and swelled, exerting great force when confined, until *click!* that lock opened slick as you please.

"Just like Rob Roy escaping through the thin air from Edinburgh castle!" he said. "Climbed out of the window right over old Fossbender's bed. Got my horse and rode from town. I had it all planned, and that's why I didn't want you hanging around."

There was a big unanswered question: how did he manage to get out the window without ripping off the mosquito net? I didn't bring that up to him, but I did to Preacher Harlow, who scoffed and averred that he'd escaped by corrupting Fossbender with liquor. The jailer had let Rusty come and go pretty much at will, only taking his boots away from him so he'd be barefoot when using the privy, etc., and on the fateful night Rusty had given him a flat pint to drink all by himself. However, it seemed to me that the liquor theory was too complicated, simple as it seemed. I'd been there in the morning and failed to detect the smell of the arisen drunk, which is one of the rankest and foulest smells there is. No, what Rusty had done was give him money. A hundred dollars would look very big to a man such as Fossbender, drawing down no more than forty per month. Two hundred would be the end of the rainbow.

As I recall that morning scene, Lee Dougherty thought the same thing!

We set off for town, in the ink of night. A few stars, a cloudy moon. Heat lightning along the horizon. Rusty and I led the way, the Irons boys stirrup to stirrup! Then came Ringbone and Preacher, and Ponds and McClure, the two new fellows, all rather spread out, to each his own. This is the safest thing to do. We didn't expect any trouble, but safe travel should be a policy. We rested at the old Post Cabin, which had been built for the mail carriers, and got to Steele about midafternoon.

All quiet. The town lay without a move under the late summer sun. The next big action would be the beef roundup. A sign saying, OUT TO DINNER hung by a chain across the Security Bank door, which was nonetheless open. Cash locked up, of course. You heard a great deal about robbery and crime in the West, but actually it was far more honest than many civilized parts. In Steele few doors were locked at night. You could walk into a store and find not a soul there, and you were expected to help yourself and leave the money. You could open the cash drawer and make change. No dwelling was ever locked, so far as I know. Out in the country you were expected to walk in and cook your supper, but woe betide those who didn't clean up the dishes and fill the wood box afterward. You'd be deemed outcast. They'd declare the hue & cry.

We rode down main street just about like we'd ridden across the prairie, Rusty and I center, the rest falling behind, and Ringbone in the drag about two horse lengths because he was a famous shot.

Not a thing happened. A number of people came forth and looked at us, but not a hand was lifted. They just watched us ride past. No sheriffs out, nobody posted on the roofs with rifles, nothing. From the Buffalo Horn stepped Funderhide. He had been awaiting our arrival. Rusty handed him a document.

"Has this been witnessed?" he asked in a ringing voice.

"It has!" says Rusty.

"I see it has been signed by T.S. Gregory. Is this how he is listed on the rolls?"

"It is!"

They were making a public announcement which is, I have been told, of force in the common law. T.S. Gregory was owner of the Anchor Brand, previously mentioned, and what Rusty had done was buy the steers, dead and alive, skinned and with their hides on, knocking their charge of grand larceny right into a cocked hat. What fools they were to go for that instead of rebranding or brand alteration, both of which might still have stood up. Oh, you had to get up early in the morning to outsmart that twain, Rusty and Funderhide!

"Where's the Hon. Lee F. Dougherty?" asked Rusty.

"In his office, I believe."

"We're in luck. The government attorney awaits." I was going to stay behind, but Rusty said no, he wanted me to witness it so I could tell Ma he wasn't a thief. We crossed over to a two story building known as the I.O.O.F. Temple, climbed some stairs, and there in the hall stood Dougherty with a double-barrel shotgun.

Naturally this brought us to an abrupt halt.

"Stand where you are!" said Dougherty, loud to cover the tremble in his voice. I won't say he was scared, just very excited.

"Now, Lee," said Funderhide, "put that weapon down; this is a lawful visit."

"What are they doing armed?" pointing to Rusty and me.

"That can be corrected. The boys can drop their guns."

I would have, I suppose, and it might have been a terrible mistake, but Rusty said "No," to me, and he said to Dougherty, "Go back in your office, Lee. You put the gun aside and we'll come in unarmed."

(You must never reach for a gun, when somebody has the drop because it will give him a chance to kill you in self defense, and if a law officer ever says, "hand me your gun," you must lift your hands and say, "You take it," and let him.)

"How about that gang out in the street?"

"Now, Lee, those are just cowboys," said Funderhide. "They're the working men of the land."

So that's how we worked it out; Rusty and I dropped our guns and we went in finding Dougherty was seated behind his desk with the shotgun leaning against the wall. Funderhide said, "That might have been prevented but for the totally unconscionable actions by other parties out of and beyond our control."

He was trying to give Lee Dougherty an easy way out.

"Here, now, is the bill of purchase, witnessed, dated long before, as you can see, delivery by parties, Butler and Crowfoot," but Dougherty was not so easily mollified.

"Why were they bearing a Snake S brand?"

"They weren't, that's the whole point! Parties delivering to Mrs. Irons so stated, but they were in error, or had intention to deceive," and so on, the attorney not listening.

"You escaped from custody, a felony!" he says to Rusty.

Well, it just seemed to take Rusty's breath away!

"Lee, I did no such thing!"

"What the h- - - are you talking about? I visited the empty jail myself! *He* visited it!" pointing to me. "And I'd still like to know how you did it!"

"I didn't do anything, Lee. As the Lord is my judge, I was *locked out.* I went to the privy, and was there a while, it was just dark, and they went and locked the door on me! I hammered and yelled but I couldn't raise a soul, so, what was I to think? Put yourself in my place. I was excluded, cut adrift—"

"Sent to Coventry," said Funderhide.

"Exactly. I was locked out in the night. I had to assume it was intentional. What would you have done? I left town."

Well, by the gods, Lee was believing him! All of a sudden he slapped his hand on the desk and cried, "I knew it! I knew there was something fishy! I knew that worthless jailer had something to hide!" And he says to me, "You saw it! You were there! What did I tell you at the time? He knew very well he'd locked up without checking the cell!"

It didn't occur to him that Rusty might just have given him a hundred dollars, because, if Rusty had just been to the privy would he have taken extra shirt, sox, underwear, shaving brush? The answer is a thundering NO!

He said, well, it was all water over the falls, and now that Rusty had given himself up, why, he might seek a reduction of bail, etc., but Funderhide demurred and said, no, he would prefer the charges just be dismissed, the case was badly tainted anyway; he said he was agreeable to let sleeping dogs lie, that the county had failed in protecting his client: he had been denied due process because it was well established that the purpose of incarceration was to guarantee not only the presence but the safety of the defendant, a dereliction of duty by the officers of the court, all of which his client was willing to overlook; he himself was willing to recommend that no action be taken or redress sought; and Lee pretended to be impressed, they would have to mount a regular military campaign to put Rusty back in irons, as he could tell by viewing the crew outside, armed to the teeth. especially.

So that settled that! We left with our freedom. I had my mouth all primed for a beer, but had to content

134

myself with a drink from the pipe flowing into the courthouse trough.

"Adam's ale!" said Funderhide. "Stick to it, boy, there's nothing better!"

Rusty consented that we load up with crackers and sardines which allayed our famishment on the long, homeward journey.

Chapter Thirteen

Aye, waiting is the hard part!
—*The Heart of Midlothian*

After his daughter, Grace, dearest to McKibbin's heart were the driving horses he raised. He had brought in several Kentucky gaited stallions, all bays, and bred them to the local best, training and selling the issue. One day Jere Sullivan drove up with such a purchase, a team of young geldings he had paid McKibbin a very fancy price for.

"Aye gad and agorrah!" he said in his quaint Irish manner, "fine it is to find one's self welcome at a family table!"

"And where aren't you?" Ma naturally asked; and he said "At McKibbin's." They had shunted him to the men at the bunkhouse, which might be deemed a calculated insult to a fellow rancher.

"And a fellow Irish Catolic, too!" said Ma.

"True! It saddens me. But he is long fallen away. I once regarded him a prince among men." He had married a protestant, a Presbyterian, and since consorted with members of the Masonic lodge.

"What is going on in that house?" he asked of us. "Something strange, indeed!" Sullivan had left his team, as usual, to be cared for, and started for the big house, in its grandeur, and was about to enter the gate, which was closed, when, "Halt," some little step-and-a-half fellow cried.

"He had me at gunpoint! In plain view of the big house. He was acting on orders, that was plain to see. 'Open up,' I said. 'I am here to deal with the General.' 'State your business!' was his answer. 'My business is with your master and no affair of yours.' Did he move out of the way? No, he did not. It was the first time I have stared down the barrel of a gun in all my years in the territory. 'The General is not at home.' But I could see people inside the house, watching. They have the lace curtains, and one moved. At last Skinner walked down with his stiff leg. All cripples work around the place, you know, and what do you make of that? Skinner is a bully, you know. He made out there were guests at the house, and something or other about them being timid in the rough land. It looked like a prison. Guards patrolled all night. Great hounds roamed the enclosure." He lowered his voice, although I was the only one who could overhear. "If you want my opinion it was not somebody they were trying to keep *out*, but someone they were keeping in." What he meant was they were keeping Grace a prisoner.

As a natural course I carried this to Rusty who had been spending much time at home.

"You can tell Jere he's wrong! The Carberrys are here from back East and they didn't want him in there eating with his knife. They're not keeping anybody 'prisoner.' "

It troubled him just the same. I have seldom seen him so taut drawn. Next day he rode to the mail box though it wasn't the time for delivery, and came back silent with his own thoughts.

"Hank, come in here." He sat with a pen and paper. "Do you think you could run an errand for me?"

"Of course."

"It's not exactly an errand. It's a very risky proposition, in fact. An adventure. Do you think you could sneak inside the Brigadier's with a letter?"

It startled me. Cripes! I went tight right to the roots of my hair.

"Sure, why not?" I said, managing a swagger.

"You'd better think about it."

"Hell, what's to think about? I know the layout, and I know Duke, which is probably one of the 'great hounds' Jere was talking about."

"I don't want you getting shot, little brother."

I didn't figure they'd actually shoot anybody. They had guests from back East, after all, and would hardly want them carrying that kind of a tale away with them.

"You might have to sneak inside the house. Do you remember how it was set up?"

I knew where the living room and the stairs were.

"I'll make a sketch for you. I don't think you'll need to go inside. You can lie low until dusk. They'd recognize me first thing if I tried to ride up there, but you'll be all right. They're hiring for fall. Won't pay you a second glance."

He was up late, writing the letter; I could see him bent over the table; next morning I told a lie to Ma and we rode off together until we reached the Brigadier's range. No further for Rusty. He pulled up and handed me the letter. *Miss Grace McKibbin* was penned on the outside in his beautiful Spencerian hand.

"Better be ready to eat that."

He truly meant eat it, chew it up and swaller it down!

"Whatever, nobody but Grace must get their hands on that letter!"

"They won't, I swear to it."

"You're a real brother."

It gave me a stir inside knowing he needed me. Now if I was not found wanting!

"I'll make it up to you sometime, kid."

"You already have, plenty."

He always brought me back a gift when he went to Sioux City, or Denver. The gift wasn't important, what was important was he hadn't forgotten. It showed that Ma was wrong saying he was selfish, and thought only of himself. He was a real, true brother and no mistake!

Chapter Fourteen

". . . Were the horned devil to rise and proffer me his assistance to set at liberty Cedric and the Lady Rowena, I fear I would hardly have religion enough to refuse the foul fiend's offer, and bid him get behind me."

—Ivanhoe

I departed from Rusty with a long wave of the hand, leading an extra horse. His idea. He said I ought always to have a fresh mount to larrup out in the event of trouble. I rode my faithful Five Spot; the extra horse was our mare, Sally. If turned loose she would head for home, but I also think he hoped I might bring Grace back with me.

I have already described the verdant Goose Creek valley, much of it sub-irrigated by bedrock streams which caused the creek to run here and disappear there, and render it withal one of the best ranching places in the land. Came around by the downstream route unseen through meadows and shady groves. The moon was out all afternoon, sinking toward the horizon, so it was going to be a dark night. This suited my purpose. Mallard ducks rose quacking from practically every pothole, giving away my approach, but I decided against stealth. What was so strange about a

140

lone rider with an extra horse? I could have been a wandering cowboy seeking work.

I met nobody. There were a few cattle grazing, the Brigadier's pet Herefords. The sun went down with a glorious sunset. Very quiet. Even after a soundless day you notice the silence of evening. I smelled kitchen smoke, the sort that rises when a cook pours grease in the stove for the final heat needed to boil dishwater; then I saw the roof of McKibbin's famous barn above the box-elder trees. I rode right on and put up in the last corral, which was a disused one and fine for my purpose, with water flowing through, and green grass in the trodden dirt. Relieved my horse of saddle and bit, but tied by means of a long rope, the best I could do in the event of a hurried departure. Didn't want to be forced to lasso at night (impossible) or when full of ginger in the morning. Nobody paid me the lightest heed.

Expected to be scared, but wasn't. Saw men I recognized and men I didn't. I fit right in. Season of the drifting cowboy, the saddle-weary, the riders of the grub line; time for the first trail herds; also the build-up for roundup, the *beef* roundup, or harvest; shipping time, when the money rolls in. Supper was already over and done. Somebody was playing a violin and with quite a good touch. They got to singing a religious hymn, one of Ma's favorites. Despite what Jere Sullivan said, no sign of an armed camp. The gate to the house yard was closed, however. I came to a plank laid across two rocks and sat down. Pretty soon a young fellow sat down beside me.

"Where you from?" he asked.

It was considered all right to ask where you hailed from, but not what your name was. This was Western custom.

141

"Out and around," says I. "I been here a number of years."

"I just came, myself. Arrived August ten. We brought in 380 head of long yearlings."

"Texas?"

"Nope, Nebraska."

"How'd you get past the Sioux?"

"Came by way of the Powder. No trouble. Had some face-ups with white owners."

"Well, they're the worst."

"My name's Frank Gruson."

"Irons."

Name meant nothing to him. "Gruson?" I said, "or Bruson?"

"Huh?"

"How do you spell it?"

He gave it a try, but bogged down and says, "I'm not much good at spellin'. It's not my strong point. Tate says the side of a cow is the only spelllin' book a cowboy needs."

This was a man named Rube Tate who was well known as cattle driver.

He said, "I keep gettin' the letters twisted around. They line up one way in a book and another way on a brand."

This was true and many find it confusing. Take the Lazy W, say; it looks the same as a lazy M, and there are many more instances.

"Didn't see you at grub pile," he says.

Grub pile is not a term you use at a cook house, only a cook wagon, showing the state of his education.

"Ate with Whip," says I. He didn't know who Whip was. "Whip Cotton, the boss."

The untruth served to quench his familiarity, and allowed me to move along, stay by myself. Somebody lit the lantern in the barn. A light went on in the big house, too. The boss cook was giving orders to his flunkey, cussing him out. McKibbin had more bosses than any owner in the territory—boss cook, range boss, boss detective; Fish Skinner was house boss; Sgt. Carrow was barn boss; Harvey Watson the bunkhouse chief, or top hand; a Frenchman named Campeau was his stud master; and his son was general manager. All of them expected extra pay. How he made ends meet I didn't know.

I had time to consider such things whilst the dark approached. The little hippity-hop fellow with the limp was patrolling the yard. It made him easy to recognize. Skinner, the house boss, had a limp, also, and I wondered whether this was accident, or had some purpose to it. The Brigadier could recognize them in the dark. And he could tell the one from the other because of size. Skinner was a large man, thick of shoulder. I was pondering this when a familiar voice brought me up sharp.

"—*Most certainly not!*" It was all I heard, although plain as if spoken at my elbow. It was the Brigadier. Quite to my surprise I discovered it had come all the way from the house. That was how the sound carried at just that evening hour.

"Oh, Otis!" a woman said, and laughter.

I'd never heard him called by his first name before. It was always "General," or some of the old-timers might call him "Colonel" which was his regular Army rank.

"Now, Pet, don't get my dander up!" he said.

The Carberrys still there from back East, and there was somebody called "Aunt Pet" I had heard about.

I stayed where I was and McKibbin walked up. I knew him in the dimness by his walk, very military.

He was on the small side, and hence with a military manner the more pronounced, you will see that is ever the case. The whiff of his cigar informed on him, also. I though he was headed right to me, but he passed without looking, I could have been a post, and so could have all the others, and he went in the barn.

No smoking in the barn was the rule, but it was his rule, and he broke it. Sgt. Carrow lit a lantern and they walked together. It was now my moment to get out of sight and *wait*.

"Ho-hum!" says I, having a long stretch. "Think I'll hit the hay."

Strolled toward the bunkhouse, and past. Got among some old wagons, hayracks, sleds, etc. Clumb into an old, high-sided wagon box of the prairie schooner type. It rested on an angle toward the house, its swing gear still being attached. At a twenty degree slope it allowed me to take my ease and see over the end-gate. I could see the entire upper story of the house when I lay down, and the rest of it when I propped myself up on my elbows.

I settled in for a long wait. If anybody came along I planned to say this was my choice rather than the hot and stuffy bunkhouse. The stars came out. Moon very low. The fiddle scratched for a time and stopped. Now and then voices came from the house, much different in quality than those from the men's quarters. "Oh, Ella," Grace said. Her voice plucked me like a string. I figured Ella had grabbed something she shouldn't, and Grace was trying to get it back. Then those sounds faded, the mosquitoes were getting bad—we never entirely rid ourselves of these pests until September, and the first good frost. I waited yet a long, long while until every light that was going to go out did go out. And a while longer.

"Well, here goes!" I said to myself, and got up. Climbed to the ground. I was right about the moon. It had dropped from view. It was a dark night, the darkest clear night I could remember. I could see things at a distance better than close up. I could see the buildings, but I had to grope with my feet. I could sort of smell the fence. The dogs were moving about.

"Here, Duke. Here, boy!" That wasn't me, it was the Brigadier. The startling thing was I was about to say the exact same thing.

I could hear them running around. "Seems pretty frisky tonight." It was his house boss, Skinner. "Fish" they called him on account of his chin. He had scarcely any and looked like a carp.

The Brigadier deigned not to answer. The only one of his men he seemed at all close to was Sgt. Carrow. He talked to the dogs and petted them. After a while a screen door slapped shut, and I could see his shadow against lamplight climbing the stairs. I couldn't tell where Skinner had gone. He lived with his wife on the lower floor, back. Figured he was gone, though, because the dogs prowled about.

"Duke!" says I, very low.

"Woof!"

Wrong dog, but here came Duke and he knew me. I patted him. His companion came around and stuck his nose to test my smell. It was all right, so I crawled through the fence. Made no attempt to steal in. I walked right along, even considered going in by the front door. Forthrightness may allay suspicion, but I might have met somebody. I walked around back whilst both dogs cavorted about, happy as could be. I could smell flowers and later the tomatoes and similar growing things in Chinaman's vegetable garden.

When you were a big enough rancher you were supposed to have a Chinese cook. Chinese didn't care to live away from their kind, and hence every year it seemed the Brigadier was going off to Helena, where there was a Chinatown, to hire one. They were domiciled in a separate house, as was their wont. This, too, could be smelled. Chinese like to raise pigs, chickens, ducks, etc. They save potato peelings, and make many strange foods for their own palate. There was a screened passage and a kitchen lean-to and a box elder tree. The box elder branched in a thick fork with one large limb over the lean-to. The lean-to was part of the kitchen. It housed the cookstove, keeping it apart from the main house for hot summer use. These sometimes were called summer kitchens. Whilst the dogs watched, and stood with their forefeet on the tree, wishing to foller, I climbed and lowered myself onto the kitchen roof. This had cedar shakes whereas the main house was roofed with genuine eastern slate. Took off my boots. The shakes had slivers which went rip-rip with every step, catching my wool socks. Reached a small veranda. It was a place the hired girl came out to stand when she shook out the chamber rugs. The McKibbins always had an Indian girl which they took in from the Agency to civilize. They kept running away and trying to walk home a hundred miles preferring a tipi to the finest house in the territory, and the Brigadier personally would set out in a buggy to bring them back.

I entered and was closed in by the warm and sluggard air of the house.

How the sweat poured off me! I was in a hall. This, I knew, by Rusty's description, ran the long way, north to south, with rooms on both sides. There was a lamp in a bracket at the head of the main stairs. I waited for a time, letting my pulse run down, and was able to

hear. A voice spoke, and there was a squeak of bed-
springs as some very heavy person turned over.
There was a smell of people, as in a hotel with the
transoms open. I stole along, and counted the doors,
because Rusty knew which room was hers; however,
I'd have known anyway because of her smell. It was a
perfume, which I had learned so well, from so many
letters in our mail box—only this time with more
force, greater even than it had been when I rode with
her in the early summer. It smote me, and truly
stirred me inside.

"Well, here goes!" I whispered, and I opened the
door.

Stood there for a time, having intended to speak.
However, my voice might have been heard by others.
So I went on in, closing the door behind me.

Chapter Fifteen

Red is the color o' blood as well as roses.
—Guy Mannering

My main worry was that she might be sleeping with somebody, one of the many female house guests from Helena or the East, or even Aunt Pet. However, I couldn't *smell* anyone else. Or sense anybody. Or hear them breathe. I couldn't hear a thing, or perhaps the very softest breathing. I could see the window, little more. The curtains hung like lead.

"Grace!"

It startled me—my own voice. I had the feeling that somebody else had spoken.

"Yes?" wide awake.

"You alone?"

"Yes."

"It's me, Hank. Henry Irons."

"Oh." She seemed to think this over for a time—I suppose, to gather her wits about her.

"Rusty sent me."

She got out of bed, barefoot, making the slightest sound on the carpet. She had on a nightgown and was stark naked inside, and you could tell that by sound. It certainly stirred me up. I felt as if I might swoon dead away.

She reached and touched me, just the very tips of her fingers, making sure of where I was.

"He wanted me to bring you a letter," I managed to say.

"How'd you get in?"

"I sneaked in."

"Oh. Did he get mine? My letter?"

"I don't know."

I got the letter into her hand, it was that dark, all groping, and she took it over to the window and opened it, but it was too dark to more than make out its shape.

"Was there any trouble in town?"

I didn't know what she meant, and we did a lot of talking at cross purpose, making me feel slow of wit. She meant had he settled matters with Dougherty? I already figured she had given him the money to pay for the steers.

"Oh, Hank, I'm practically a prisoner!" she cried. "They watch me all the time!"

She lit a lamp to read the letter. It was only a candle inside a chimney, but it seemed very bright, actually brilliant, and I felt like one on stage, in view of all, though of course nobody could see me from outside because of the angle. She sat down and read the letter all the way through, about three pages. She had very long, narrow white feet which stuck out from beneath her nightgown. She had the longest big toes I ever saw. She sat for a while and then put the letter away in a drawer. Blew out the candle.

"Hank?"

I was right there.

"Huh?"

"Oh, there you are!" She took hold of my hand. She pulled me along and we sat on the bed. I'm not going to try and describe how I felt. Even were I a Sir Walter Scott it would be impossible. "I want you to feel something."

I don't know what I expected. She pulled my hand right down and pressed it right against her stomach. Well, it wasn't her stomach, actually. It was lower down.

"Do you feel that?"

"Huh?" says I, or something equally dumb.

"Do you?"

"I don't know."

"Can't you guess? I'm going to have a baby."

Now that she told me I could tell there *was something*, rather firm, sort of like a mushmelon. I wondered if they knew. It would scarcely show if she wore the right clothes. It might under that tight-waisted riding skirt.

"Does he—your Pa—?"

"Yes, he does. Mrs. Skinner spies on me all the time. Then I told somebody and shouldn't have." She didn't say who. One of her friends I supposed. "I'm safe enough for now."

Safe from what?

"Papa won't do anything until after the Carberrys leave."

"What do you mean, 'won't do anything?' "

"Hank—he's taking me away."

"Where to?"

"San Francisco."

"Rusty can foller. He can't keep you locked up always."

"It will be too late."

"How come?"

"He says he'll have the baby taken care of."

Taken care of? Then it came to me what she meant.

It fairly raised my hair, the awfulness of it! People were always talking about women who were that way having the baby *taken care of.* Sometimes they said they had the kid *knocked.* It was as if they knocked it on the head and killed it, like a runt in a litter. There was an Indian woman, a regular old crone, in at Benton who was said to do the job, charging five dollars. This I'd learned by listening in on conversations.

"They can't do that!" says I. "It's against the law!"

"Yes, they can. I'm a minor and Papa can do anything he likes."

"It's a crime, ain't it?"

"He can do it. A man like Papa can do things despite the law."

Yes, that was the truth. I said, "Why, his own grandson!"

No use. She laid her hand on my arm, real gentle.

"Hank. Will you tell Rusty?"

You can bet I would, or die in the attempt!

"Tell him I'll meet him at Meadow Lark in four days," Meadow Lark being one of their secret places. "Tell him three or four. Or five, to play safe."

"All right."

"Tell him I'll try to get some money."

I suppose she meant she'd snig it from her father, but I didn't ask. I set my mind to remembering every single thing she said.

Somebody was up, moving around. A heavy step descended the stairs. You could *feel* it rather than hear it. She held onto me, and we listened.

"It's Uncle Phil. He has to get up with his asthma."

Soon a terrible smell assailed us. He was burning medicinal leaves. We listened and listened but nobody else could be heard. Grace stood so quiet! and then by accident her bare foot touched mine.

"Why, Hank, you haven't any shoes on!" into my ear.

"Left 'em on the kitchen roof," I muttered.

It embarrassed me to be caught with the toes out of my sox. All my sox were home knit and Ma would darn them, and weave in new toes, but finally they got too far gone and she'd give up. They'd be sort of like tunnels. You could put them on from either end, actually, only the heel might fit wrong. You could fold over and sort of grab with your toes and put them on in that manner, after which they fit all right. Served for hot weather.

She kept feeling around my toes with hers, and finally she ran her little, long, cool foot right in beside mine. It was like a weasel wiggling into a hole. How it stirred me!

"Hank!" she says, and she started to cry. "Oh, Hank, I've been so alone!"

I had to comfort her. Awkward at it, big and clumsy, and she so fine and frail; I patted her and she clung to me, and she sobbed right in my ear, which got full of slobber.

"Do you think I'm a wicked, wicked girl?" she asked.

The answer to that was, no I didn't! I thought she was the gentlest creature on all the earth.

She said she and Rusty were married already in the name of truth, and their baby was a proof of their love, etc., and she didn't want me to think bad of her, and she ran her hands up inside my shirt, and sort of swooned, and there we were on the bed, fortunately, because otherwise it would've been the floor, and she said, "Oh, Hank, your belt buckle!"

It hurt her and I let her unfasten it, and what happened then was sort of a dream, like falling into an abyss, endless, where you couldn't stop and didn't want to. "Stop!" I recall her saying, "Hank, you'll *hurt* yourself!" And she said, "Here, let me show you," and I did, because she had had more experience. She took me in hand, as it were, and all of a sudden it was the most natural thing in the world. I make a point of this, using the word *natural* with advisedness, as in "nature," because Ma says that people who give in to this temptation of the flesh are going to be damned; they are headed for Gehenna as night follers day; but I say, no! she is wrong! and that God Almighty would never have made anything so wondrous if he hadn't meant it to happen. Those were my sentiments at the time, and they remain my sentiments still. May the chips fall where they may!

I was in most awful jeopardy because what if the Brigadier came walking in? But despite this a "peace that passeth understanding" descended on me. Actually fell asleep, or deep doze. Remained where I was, in the saddle as it were. "No, you're not heavy at all," she said. And she said, "Oh, I've been so lonesome. But don't say a word about it to Russell, will you?" She could bet on that! "It's all right, because you're his brother, but he might not understand, etc." And, "You're lying right on your nephew!" And she laughed a little, and licked my ear, etc., and she said I could do it some more, but real gentle, I was so big and strong, etc.

"Hank!"

Grace, with whispered alarm, startled me awake. "Hank! It's morning!"

It wasn't, actually. It was the gray before dawn. But did I hop out of there in a hurry! And, "Cock-a-doodle-doo!'' the clarion call of old Chanticleer, the China-man's white rooster, hustled me on my way.

No fond goodbyes. She stayed in bed and I, after a peek into the hall, made exit. No movement any-where, all still, the lamp burning dim, no odor of hackbark smoke, or whatever it was, that uncle so-and-so breathed for his asthma. I moved quickly to the veranda, down to the kitchen roof; thence, boots in hand, to the shadowy ground scorning the box elder tree. ''Cock-a-doodle-doo! Cock-a-doodle-doo!'' The rooster kept summoning the hens to get up and scratching, because day was at hand; but as yet no sign of life in the kitchen, or down at the men's cook-house, no fire, no whack of axe breaking kindling, no watchmen, not even the dogs; only I, moving like a wraith, across the yard and around the buildings, qui-eting an urge to run. It was half a mile at the very least. A chill mist hung over the creek where it ran through the corrals; it was too dark to see, but the sudden quiet of frogs on my approach told of mud and water; I skirted, climbed pole fences, and got to the right corral, which was the last one, and my horses waited.

All was well. I moved about, and they stood to be haltered. I had a bridle and a bit but chose not to use it. It was your common hinge bit, no curb or port, but for all that a horse will fight it, hence one is much bet-ter off using just a halter, or in this case a hackamore, which is actually a bridle without the bit, only a borsal of braided rawhide. Also saddled but lightly cinched. Treat your horse the way he likes to be treated and likewise will he you. I was giving the well-worn latigo its final cross and pull when a man seemed to rise up from the ground. He'd come over the corral but with such an easy movement, and not a sound! Gad! how it startled me!

I let my pounding heart run down and stood with my horse between. He was a stranger, a very lean thirty-odd. No smell at all. You can almost always get a whiff of a bunkhouse, looked as if he scorned not only a night's sleep but houses in general. No gun on him. This meant he probably wasn't one of the new guards, but a visitor, who by custom kept their guns in their warbags. He was probably a trail herder, one who slept with one eye open for reasons of his own; we got some very hard types every year in the season.

"Leaving early," he remarked.

Not a question, it wouldn't have been proper manners.

"Yep!" says I, a short answer, but sufficient. Ask me no questions and I'll tell you no lies. I mounted holding the lead line. This placed him with the obligation of opening the gate, i.e. lowering the corral bar.

He just stood there and we had sort of a face-off. Wondered if I'd have to ask, but he, with a surly and slow pace, let the pole down.

"*Gracias.*" Using the Spanish term, which for some reason seemed seemed right to the circumstance, as if I was far off and going farther. (Many Spanish words in the cattle land, and more every season, *riata* for lariat, *compañero* for companion, and *fuga lay,* the "fugitive law," whereby they can leave the jail door open and shoot you when you walk out. If you're ever in jail in Old Mexico this is a good thing to know; it might save your life.)

So, out and away! Free of fences at last I had a good gallop, was able to breathe at last, clear my head. So much had happened I needed a spell of the wide and open. Dawn arrived, and hot morning, with sweat and thirst, but I was my own person again. There's nothing like the long lonesome to give you a *view*, not only of the eye but of the mind. I was able to sort out events, put them in proper importance. Although I hadn't brought Grace with me—I figured it was why Rusty wanted me to take the extra horse, just on the odd chance—but I had visited her, and on nearly all scores he'd be obliged to admit that my journey was a *success!*

With leisure I was able to look at things from his point of view, and hers, and from the Brigadier's. Especially the latter's. When you came down to cases the Brigadier would call the tune; if he said "go" then it would be go. As of that moment the relatives only were delaying him. But time was short, growing shorter. Very soon her condition just *had* to be noticed —tomorrow by Aunt Pet, day after that by the Chinaman, and the one after that by the boys at the bunkhouse. And, oh! wouldn't they be happy. People are truly vile in their envy and the joy they take in another's shame. The same people who would jump in the river and save your life will chortle with glee if you get caught with your pants down, as the saying goes. And of course somebody like the Brigadier, who presumed to be the lord of the land! I could just hear them. "How about the big boss, sends all the way to Kentucky to get sires for his bay mares but I see our local range stallions are good enough for his girl!" "Rad-headed one, I understand!" (Ha-ha, ha-ha-ha!) "Understood he took his daughter off to Californy to git her kid knocked. That's what the stage driver told me. Said they had her laced down like Ada Menken in *Mazeppa*, but it showed."

Got to computing how much time he might have. I figured I knew when the child was made, or conceived, as they say. The time of a woman with child is nine months. Nine months and two days to be exact. I knew this to be a proven fact because of something that had happened in at Fort Steele:

There was a saloonkeeper there named Coon Corley who was a bachelor. Not an unusual condition, our territory boasts only one woman to every two and a half men, and as a result the matrimonial clubs are very active, and advertise in all the papers. You are asked to subscribe to a magazine called Cupid's Bower, and Coon sent off through this organ and got himself a wife. He had her picture and showed it all around. As a result, when she got off the stage everybody was on hand to make her welcome, see they got married, and they gave them a party and free dance, and afterward a shivaree, where they beat on tin pans and blow horns under the newlyweds' window, etc., so the date was well marked, and nine months and two days later she delivered to Coon a bouncing baby boy, and people all joked with him saying, "How come you were six hours late?" they asked. "Explain yourself, Coon. Why the delay?" the birth having been at about noon.

As a matter of fact you can't tell *right to the hour*, but nine months and two days is established. So you see what the Brigadier was up against! Not that I was excusing what he intended to do. But I understood what moved him.

With these thoughts and many others I rode home.

Chapter Sixteen

He sate her on his milk-white steed.

—Waverley

"Y ou didn't get the letter delivered!" was how Rusty greeted me. "I knew damn well you wouldn't be up to it."

"I did, too! I even got in and talked to her."

This mollified him some.

"Did she send any answer?"

"She didn't put anything down."

He waited to hear what it was, very impatient.

"She told me she was going to have a *baby!* And it was *yours.*"

Naturally this didn't surprise him, but he looked at me with a sort of smile to see how I took it.

"She said her father knew about it."

He took that calmly, too. In fact, I had the feeling he took some pleasure. How he hated the Brigadier! For the whipping, of course, but before that because of the time he rode over to pay a visit carrying the bouquet of sweet flags, and had been driven off, called "shanty trash," etc, while people were listening. Then an ugly thought came to me: he had *wanted* to get her with child just to strike McKibbin where it hurt the most!

"He's taking her away to San Francisco." I didn't

wait for him to ask why but went straight on. "She says he intends to have the baby tooken care of."

"*Tooken* care of? what do you mean by that?" he ripped out.

"Well, that's what they call it. He aims to have the baby *knocked.*"

He went absolutely pallid. Under his brick-red tan you could see his freckles, and all the little blemishes of his face. He actually turned on me with fists doubled so I had to sidle out of the way. He seldom cursed, but he did now, and named the Brigadier some things I'd never care to set down on paper. He named McKibbin every foul and dastardly thing he could think of. Finally he ran down and said in a hoarse voice, "Where is she?"

"At home. I sneaked in. Clumb up the tree and kitchen roof—"

"They didn't see you? You're sure?"

"Yes, I'm sure. The Carberrys are there visiting from back East and she'll be safe until they go. He doesn't want them to find out. They're her mother's relations—"

"I know the Carberrys."

"Well, she says she wants to meet you and can be at Meadow Lark, and you'd understand."

"When?" He was ready to leave right that minute.

"Three or four days. Or five."

"Three to *five*?"

"That's what she said. It depends on if she can slip away."

"Did she say anything about money?"

"Yes, she did, but she wasn't sure what she could get."

"All right. You did fine." He was sorry now the way

he'd come down on me. "I still need your help, Hank. I don't know what I'd ever do without you."

What he set out to do was gather every hoof of horse stock he owned, or owned partially, and put me and the boys to that task. I could see his plan. You can drive horses a good long way, and sell them. Unlike cattle that have to go to the Eastern market, and pass the brand books, horses can be disposed of at any number of horse auctions. The Army buys them, also the freighters and the miners, and unlike a cow it's not illegal to rebrand. Lots of horses get traded so often their sides, flanks and shoulders look like a brand book. It was his plan to head out with Grace and all the horses he could drive, their fortune on the hoof—and if there's a better way to put distance under you than with a band of horses I don't know it!

He left to keep his appointment at Meadow Lark and came back two days later looking very peaked. He wouldn't tell me a thing, but went to bed, in the hot lateness of the afternoon.

"What's the matter with your brother?" Ma wanted to know. "Is the law after him again? What's he gathering all them horses for?"

"Ask *him!*"

"Don't give me any of your sass! I ask because I wanted to *know* and I got a right to know!" etc., showing how things went for me. Hard indeed is the lot of the youngest child!

Then something else happened and it turned Rusty into, if not a crazy man, then a good imitation thereof:

"Go get the mail," Rusty says to me.

He thought maybe she'd get a chance to write him a letter, but not so. I waited for Summerfelt, the mail driver, who had naught for us but some papers.

160

"Where's Rusty?" he says.

I figured it was no business of his where he was, and I could see there was something he was just itching to impart.

"Guess he ain't likely to see more of that sprightly girl of General McKibbin's."

"How's that?"

"Left the country. Took the coach to Three Forks, and were they ever riding herd on her!"

"Who was?"

"*They* was, the General and the Skinners."

Naturally I hustled right back to tell Rusty with the results heretofore described. He went flinging and cursing around, blooding his fist on the wall, etc., and then as sudden became deadly calm.

"Summerfelt told you that? How would he know they were riding herd on her? It's not the General's way to make any show to the likes of Summerfelt. It's gossip. They're still in town."

How he knew they must still be in town was Summerfelt saying the Three Forks Coach. It only went once a week. It was the Benbow Line and was not only once per week, on a Friday, but often as not a day late. It could leave a day late but not a day early because it had a mail contract.

"Of course they'd take the Three Forks coach! It's exactly what McKibbin would do. He wouldn't dare take the Big Horn coach for fear some of his Helena society folks would be on the train."

What he meant was the Northern Pacific Limited. The Three Forks coach went over the Snowy Range directly to the new spur line of the Utah & Northern, and south on that narrow gauge line to the U.P. at Corrinne, Utah.

"It means we still have time, little brother."

He went about sorting his things. Gave me his shot-gun, a genuine Damascus barrel double. "Yours to keep." Guess he didn't think it likely he'd ever come back. Gave me a set of spurs, some hair chaps, a rifle and pistol. The rifle was calibre .38 and flung a bullet almost as big as Ma's old Buffalo Sharps. The pistol was a Colt in the new .41. He never wanted a gun like anyone else had. Never carried a cartridge belt. "You hit the mark with what's in the magazine and that will be sufficient," he liked to say. Rusty was a fine marksman, but not so good as Cecil who was shot in Wyoming, so figure that out.

He put some things in an alligator skin valise and some in a war-bag. It was sunset by then, but he was not to delay. We were leaving to catch the Benbow coach.

"Where you going?" asked Ma, but she knew I wasn't going to say, and that it was no use to argue. So many things had happened to her that she just sort of gave up. Even while I stood there she took to muttering about Hoffner running his steers on our Organ Pipes Range.

"Maybe he'd doing the right thing"—meaning Rusty—"to just leave and be done with it." Gave me a sack of doughgods, the so-called hardtack of the Army.

"Good-bye," I said. "I'll see you in four or five days."

Rusty never said good-bye or anything.

It was quite a herd of horses to set off with at that hour. Ardis went with us until we were well started.

"Well, good-bye," he says. "Don't step in any badger holes."

Had the strange feeling I'd never see him again.

162

There was much lightning and a smell of rain, and you could feel the electricity in your hair, and the way your shirt stuck to your back. Also the glow of the horses, turning them into lightning rods.

"It'll clear," said Rusty. "This is a dry moon right now. We'll get no heavy rains until the equinox."

It cleared off and the moon shone. It was hard keeping tabs on the horses because, like all the Irons stock, they ran to dapples and light roans. The Irons stock were famous since the gold rush days when Pa came here driving two hundred head he'd bought off the Flathead Indians. The steamboats would put up against the shore where the freighters would take over for the last leg to Alder Gulch. On good seasons the boats got all the way to Fort Benton, where there was a fair road down to the camps, but more often it was impossible, and they'd find some spot on the south shore to unload, and that was that. The freighters had to find their own road, and many the harrowing tales of their troubles. Those flathead horses wouldn't have known a road if they'd seen one. As packhorses they'd carry 300 pounds per animal. Oh, they put up a fight! But fastened nose to tail they'd soon learn who was boss, and Pa said by the time they reached Alder they were *broke horses*, and could be sold as draft stock at an average of ten ounces in gold, per team. Then back again with a few of his lead and drag stock to do the same thing over again. He made a lot of money, and was doing what he loved, working with horses. Both the Wildhorse Spring and the Wildhorse Hills were named for him, not him for them, as some suppose. He put us *on the map*, as they say.

We slept and were awakened by the hot sun. The horses had drifted. We gathered them and drove to

Mapes Station, abandoned. This whole country was now controlled by Enterprise Land & Cattle. The grass was good because they were saving it for winter range. Using Irons' range, Ma might say. Mapes's was on the old freight road. The once proprietor, "Silky" Mapes, had been shot in a quarrel and was buried with others in a little fenced square. Slept under the sagebrush. You could see where gophers had dug holes down into the graves. Not a happy sight. Glad to go on, climbing over a great bulge where you had a view of basins and mountains, the Snowies, Big and Little Belts, others.

Spent a long and hungry night with only hard doughgods to munch.

"That's the new Benbow station on Dead Woman Creek," says Rusty, next midday.

I couldn't make it out, took him at his word. Sure enough, in time the buildings took shape in the heat wave. On a road, now. No tracks since the last rain, most of which had dried away. The station was on a dry creek with a well. It was run by a man and wife, both foreigners. It was their job to keep fresh horses on hand when and if a coach arrived, and feed the passengers. They had a son of about ten and feeble-minded. He tagged me around and tried to make friends. Couldn't talk but would beat his elbows to his sides and crow like a rooster. A pitiful case, but happy for all that.

Found out the stage was a day late. We ate salt pork and johnnycake at a cost of 50 cents each, but watered all our stock free, at the well. Creek dry, everything parched, we were having the driest and the hottest summer in years. The sunsets splendrous! Born and reared in that land, one never got tired of looking at the sunsets.

Resaddled, on fresh mounts, then slowly away. No hurry now. We watched for the Benbow coach. We were on a long, slow climb. Foothills of the Snowy Range. Greener grass, new smells, and soon a creek with cool water.

"You aim to camp here?"

Didn't even answer. A very aggravating man. You think he'd at least answer a simple question. There was an old stage station that nobody lived in. Beyond that was a canyon, not the sort with solid rock walls, but steep and rocky. The road crossed the creek and crossed it and crossed it. Lost track how many times. The horses were ahead of us, held in by the mountain-sides, and you could tell by the roily water when they stirred up the creek. They were my task whilst Rusty rode away up on a shoulder of ground to survey with his spyglass.

I knew when he came down what he'd seen. He didn't have to tell me more than by the grimness of his visage.

"We'll have to find a place to hold those horses," he says.

We were in good luck there. The canyon fell away on one side, less rock and timber, a mountain sag where grass and plants grew high as a horse's knees, but of strange nature to them: they had to try out this and that and compare it with the prairie grass back home. Then they'd snort from the smell.

Rusty sat around and watched, and watched, and chewed on pieces of grass as if he had the whole week at his disposal. Finally he deigned to say, "No hurry, kid. They have just a *single team*. You know how stingy Benbow is. I can't see how they expect to pull this pass at all, a mud wagon and just *one single team*."

We had plenty of time, of course. You could see nothing or hear nothing. Stood and listened to our heartbeats, and after that a stillness. It was a ringing stillness, the mountain quiet being different from the quiet of the plains. This comes from the echo which is ever there, from rock faces, and the stream. Out of the plains the sounds fly off into space, the earth being round. The mountains are like putting your ear to the hole in a guitar. On the quietest night you can hear the roar of the wind in timber.

Finally we rode back to the road. Tied our mounts out of any possible view, and armed ourselves to the teeth. He had some stuff to disguise himself with, but not I.

"You're going to be up on the mountainside. They won't see you at all. Just your hat and the barrel of the thirty-eight."

This was the rifle, a regular cannon, as heretofore set down.

He seemed to know right where he was going. There was a place where it looked as if the road had been blasted from the mountainside with giant powder. From time to time rocks had fallen and had to be cleared away. There was a steep drop to the creek, so the road was much constricted. He directed me above to roll down some more rocks. Not too many, just what would look like a natural fall, and would force them to stop and roll them out of the way.

"They won't suspect a thing," said Rusty. "Some coach lines would, but not Benbow. No gold, no Army contract, no soldier's pay, nothing. Nobody in his right mind would rob a Benbow coach," etc.

There was a place above where I was supposed to hide with just the rifle showing. This was an old dead-fall, a real king of the mountain in its day, but now so rotted you could run your foot in to the ankle, all red crumble under the shell. However, rocks had slid down and been stopped and these would protect me from bullets. He made me get down and do this and that, and finally he said it was all right. About then the coach was coming.

"What am I supposed to do? What's the plan?"

He just laughed and said, "You can't map the river till you've been down it, kid. Loose plan for loose situations." And that was that.

Rusty got out of view, and pretty soon here it came, with just a single team, although a heavy one. The coach was one of those light "six-fours," i.e. it was called six-passenger but held four. A mud wagon, no doors. Openings but nothing to close. Windows, no glass. A woman's fat arm in view. That would be Mrs. Skinner, who spied on Grace. The driver was a little fellow of about 110 pounds. Benbow hired them small as possible so as to leave more room for pay load. Fish Skinner sat beside him. All dressed up in suit, collar, suspenders. Had his coat off holding it. Had a shotgun between his knees.

"Whoa!" says the driver.

"What's wrong?" asked McKibbin. Would have known the ring of that voice anywhere!

Fish leans over and says, "Rocks in the road," through the window.

McKibbin started to get out the far side, and just then Rusty rose beside the road.

"Hands up!"

Seemed to appear from nowhere. Looked monstrous. Had a blanket and gunny sack on, and his hat. Pistol in hand.

Now here I made a mistake. Rather, I failed to do something I should have. I should have let them know they were tooken from two sides. Hence Fish, thinking he was out of Rusty's view, tried to come up and a round with his shotgun.

"Halt!" cried I belatedly, and gad! I pulled the trigger.

Bang! went the thirty-eight so close it deafened me. Seemed to tear my face off. I must have shot to frighten. Pure instinct. At any rate he stood at the same instant, and outlandish as this may seem, the bullet cut right through his suspenders, where they crossed in the back, and his pants fell down!

It wouldn't have happened again in a hundred years. He must have had a lot of silver money, or some shotgun shells in his pockets to pull them down. They simply dropped *flop!* and there he stood in his underwear. I have had many a chuckle over this since, but I was not laughing *then!*

"Clem! Clem!" Mrs. Skinner was yelling, and the horses went stamping around, and the driver geehawing over rocks and managed to stop at a tilt. Luckily the Brigadier was flung around, and if he had a gun was unable to use it, because I dare say Rusty, for all his vindiction, would not care to shoot him down before his daughter's eyes.

Then out she came, Grace, quick as a rabbit. I wondered had she been forewarned, but that couldn't have been. She had heard Rusty's voice and guessed the remainder.

"You, Skinner! Hand down the baggage."

Skinner complied, if one-handed, holding up his pants.

"Not that! Just the young lady's baggage."

There were some other things said. The Brigadier had charge of his voice and said something to which Grace answered, "No, Papa, I'm going with him."

So that settled that! In a shorter time than you might think possible the coach was on its way once more.

"Driver! Turn around!" McKibbin was saying. "Turn around, I say! We're returning to Fort Steele!"

It would have been a hard thing to do, anyway, but the driver was deaf to command. He wasn't close to turning—he was just whipping that team out of gun range.

"Oh, Hank, you were wonderful!" said Grace.

"That's my brother!" said Rusty. "See how he shot old Skinner's pants right off him?"

I was in a hustle to put distance under us before the General came back with his cohorts, but Rusty couldn't show more unconcern. The three of us walked to where the horses were, using the saddles to balance the luggage, which included a small trunk.

"Evening!" says Rusty, breathing the air. "The finest time of the day!" etc.

Grace had to repack, leaving the trunk, and put things on a packhorse. She needed no help from anyone where horses were concerned. A real equestrienne. He used his own saddle for her, shortening the stirrups. Chose old Maccabee for her, and a big bay named Drifter for himself, fitting him with surcingle and hackamore, Indian style.

"You take the saddle."

This suited me fine, having no fondness for bareback, while Rusty often did it through choice. Built for it, like many an Indian, long-legged, loose as rags, and far forward where he could guide a horse suitable by the press of his knees.

"Hey! ain't you taking the horses?"

"No, we're leaving them for you, little brother."

So that was good-bye. They left with only Maccabee, Drifter and a packhorse. I sure felt lonesome. I had a terrible, empty feeling as if she had abandoned me. The quiet of the mountainside then made itself heard. That is, I could hear the insects waking with evening, and all the sounds of a strange country, that aren't true sounds, but differences. And there were the smells that come when the sun passes and the shadows grow. I could smell strange plants, and I could smell Grace. Yes I could, it wasn't just memory—because there lay her kerchief. Was it by accident she dropped it, or had she left it for me in remembrance? I took it and tucked it inside my shirt, next to my heart. Then I set off, driving the horses. This was easy. They always go well when homeward bound.

Chapter Seventeen

When the last laird of Ravenswood to Ravenswood shall ride.

—Bride of Lammermoor

I asked myself the question, why had Rusty gone to all the bother with the horses and then rode off with only the three? Did he want me to leave the wide trail for the pursuers to foller? If so, well enough, it was a role I was willing to take. Gathered the herd and set off for home. Made no attempt to hide my trail. It would have been impossible, anyhow. Made it out of the hills during twilight. Camped alongside the creek. Watched for the returning stagecoach. It did not appear. Up at the dawn. Horses were eating real well, not so their herdsman. I was wolf-hungry, yet made wide avoidance of the stage station on Dead Woman Creek. Left Grace's kerchief hung to a sage where it would flutter bright in the sun. Figured the Brigadier might find it, or his henchmen.

"Come foller me, General!" I shouted, with an errant laugh in the face of fate. "Come you and your minions and I'll take you on a ride you'll never forget!"

Could have got home easy enough, but I took a long swing into the badlands. Logical for Rusty to seek protection in one of the outlaw towns along the river. Badlanders country. I lost my way and found it and lost it again. The herd melted away, a horse here, a horse there, to return to the home range in the fullness of time. Bullberries were ripe. The prairie chickens feasted on them, get their crops so full they couldn't fly and you could kill them with a stick. They feasted on bullberries and I feasted on them. Wolf-hungry I could eat as many as three prairie chickens at a meal, roasted, without salt. I'd by now lost all track of time. I had but my own mount and three of the herd left. Now at last, I turned toward the home ranch.

All seemed peaceful. More than peaceful, it was deserted. The chickens hadn't been fed. "Hey!" I yelled inside the house, getting no answer, expecting none. Flies buzzed against the window. She'd taken the Sharps. No sign of the buggy. I kept yelling, "Hey! is anybody around?" until at last Dad came from the cook house and stood blinking.

"Oh, that you, Hank?"

"Yes."

He acted sort of wild. "Are you alive?"

"Of course I'm alive."

"They said you'd been hung, you and Rusty, over on Forty Mile."

Cripes! how it scared me. Could it be they'd captured him? Forty Mile was in the direction he might have gone, over near the Moccasin Range.

"When?"

"Why, three or four days. They hung you and Rusty both. Rannow said so. He came especial to see your Ma."

"Well, as you can see Rannow didn't know what he was talking about."

"I known him fifteen year and *he does too* know what he's talking about!"

"Are you trying to tell me I been hung? What's this in front of you, a spirit?"

"There've been stranger things!"

Ye gods, he meant it! He was a sort of purple in the face, and more than just an old man's color. He was afraid.

"I'm all right. Come and feel of me. Take hold."

He edged up and did so, and seemed satisfied.

"Yes, you're in the flesh, all right. Whew! that was a relief! But they hung Rusty, and that is certain."

He *wanted* them to. Rusty had always been hard on him. Case of the old dog wanting to bark over the young dog's grave.

"Preacher and Ringbone said the same."

"Where's Ma? She hear that news?"

"No, she'd already gone off in the buggy. There's been hell to pay around here, let me tell you! Posse riding all over the place. Casey Hobbs was here. Wiggin, he had on a deputy U.S. Marshal badge. Ed Peale, Long Henry, all that gang. Wanted to serve some sort of an attachment. It was 'an order to show cause.' Casey Hobbs tried to get her to accept it, but she wouldn't let him near the house. He was about to walk right in there anyhow, but *whang!* she took a shot at him."

"She shot at Casey Hobbs?"

"Oh, did he jump! They all went a-scramblin, but they didn't shoot back. Tom Ward acted like it was pretty funny, but he hid like everybody else. Your ma shouted about trespass, and she had a right to protect her property, and they better make tracks, but they didn't. They just stayed clear of the house."

"Where were the men?"

"Our fellows? They stayed clear, and Hobbs told them they'd better make tracks if they know what was good for them. He said this was a rustler's lair. He said they'd be accomplices. He nailed up a notice, he nailed it right to the old bell post, and Ma came out and tore it down. Finally they left and I went up there and tried to talk with her. She acted like she didn't even see me. At night I heard her talking, and talking, and I figured you'd come home, but there wasn't a soul there. That is, nobody that *could be seen*. Do you know who she was talkin' to? She was talkin' to your pa!"

"I hope she wasn't getting an answer," I said, sort of a weak joke, but Dad Walsh didn't know it was a joke. He said,

"Of that I'm not so sure. It wasn't that I heard him, but I could *feel* him," and more of that nature.

"Oh, to hell with that!" and I realized I said it just like Rusty.

"I'm just telling you. I was here and you weren't. It got dreadful cold. The weather wasn't so cold, but a chill passed through me as made me nearly shake my clothes off. Well, I went to bed finally, and woke up late. I didn't get up until about nine, and Ma was just driving off in the buggy."

"Where to?"

"I don't know. The upper road."

"When did Ardis and Robins leave?"

"They left before the sheriff did. Then they come back and started mooching around, thinking I should feed them, even though they said they had quit, and they wanted to get paid. Then Rannow came, as I

174

said. And Preacher, and Ringbone, wanting to find out about Rusty. They certainly went pale in the face when I told them you'd been hung, you and him, over at Forty Mile. That's where it was, wasn't it?"

"Where I was hung?"

"Yah."

You can see how crazy he was. Then he started telling about what Preacher and Ringbone had told him, that there was a lot of shooting over at Eighty-Eight Coulee.

"Maybe that's where you were hung and not on the Forty Mile." He was asking me if that's where I'd been hung! He says, "The Preacher thanked me for a job well done. 'We're counting on you to hold the fort, Dad,' he says to me. Ringbone said the same. By God, nobody ever accused me of quitting when the going got rough. In for a penny, in for a pound, that's me!"

True enough, he was the only one of our men that had stuck by us.

Chapter Eighteen

For three wild lads were we, brave boys
And three wild lads were we;
Thou on the land, and I on the sand,
And Jack on the gallows tree!

—Guy Mannering

I'd looked forward to a good rest at the old home ranch, but none was vouchsafed me. I ate and set forth follering Ma's wheel tracks. They seemed headed toward the Stamp place, so I swung off and climbed to the Organ Pipes rocks, which was the main summit, to see if I could spot her, or the buggy.

I couldn't figure out what was going on, and needed to get off by myself. What did this posse have to do with it? Why weren't they out beating the badlands for Rusty and Grace? Could it be that two gangs were down on us, Hoffner on the one hand and McKibbin on the other?

"Hold on, Irons!" I said. (I'd got in the habit of talking to myself out on the long lonesome—kept me from going batty.) "McKibbin never did foller your false trail to the badlands. You spent upwards of a week to no avail. When he got that stagecoach turned around he went straight and enlisted all possible aid, which included the interests which wanted to cut up the Irons range. How better to make Rusty show himself than by turning us out of home? It was a variation on the ruse used when they arrested Ma. They were up to their old tricks. Naturally the General didn't show himself. No, not he, it was likely to cause scandal. It would besmirch the noble name."

Easy riding, keeping watch in all quarters, I got to the Organ Pipes toward late afternoon. Many times have I mentioned this famed landmark. It was a reef of volcanic rock weathered into columns that from afar bore resemblance to an instrument called the pipe organ. It didn't look like one close up. Actually, when you got there, you rode among a lot of knobs and pillars, all rusty and broken. You didn't have to clamber over the rocks. You could sit down and rest your back and look at the entire land, even see the river, a flat shine like knife metal when the heat wave faded, and things fined down. I could see our place and the old Stamp place equally distant. Spencer Stamp (rightly Stampp) was a steamboat engineer who homesteaded there after the war and ran mules. Later he left for the mines to engage in the smithy business and Pa bought him out for $400. He had built a good house, cache house, sheds, etc., which still looked perfectly solid from a distance, but all had fallen into disrepair, roofs full of holes, with pack rats and skunks taking over so the roundup didn't camp at the house, but used tents. Stamp Creek looked like a big one, broad and many groves, but all was subsurface water, only a trickle along the bed. They'd much rather have used our creek, but we wouldn't stand for it. Pa would have allowed it if they'd have paid, but they never agreed on a price. Away off were some dry lakes, and then a number of coulees, one of which was Tetley's Coulee where Preacher, Ringbone and the third fellow had heard shots.

Took my ease. I could hear my horse, Old Keno, which I had saddled at the ranch, going rip-rip, rip-rip, tearing off the grass. Listening for shooting. The heat faded, allowing one to hear from farther and farther away, and see better, the lines of things taking firm shape. There were some objects about a mile off which I once took to be cattle, but they weren't, they never moved. What it looked like was a recent buffalo kill. Pa had shown me one when small, and I still remembered the stink. A great convocation of magpies. No buzzards in our country, magpies serve the purpose. It was too far to be sure, but I could see something that could have been the white and jet flash of these birds, first cousin to the crow.

Was studying this when something at far greater distance caught my eye. It was movement away down on Stamp Creek, the far side, atop the cutbank rim—horsemen. I counted five, later seven. They kept dropping from sight and coming out again. A good road ran along the bottom, but they eschewed it. They seemed to be giving the brush a wide berth, and the buildings as well, when they came to them.

I watched and watched. As they angled closer (but still miles away) I was able to make out that there were seven horses, but only five riders. The thing that fooled me was that the two extra horses were saddled. You can always tell, though you can't actually see the saddles. Two empty saddles! It gave me a bad feeling. Then, *pop! pop!* the far, very far-off sound of gunfire.

It was so far there was no echo. Echoes die out while the true sound doesn't, and that's a way you can tell distance. I listened and got to hearing things like a yelling, or ringing in the ears. It might have been imagination, or it might have been coyotes. It was evening, their prime howling time, and they'd have been stirred up by the shots. There were just the two, maybe three shots, no more. Came a gigantic sunset, all furnace hues; that season had produced the greatest sunsets ever seen, and the hues remained while shadow spread across the land. The time had come for me to move, so I rode down to what looked like the buffalo kill.

Somebody had shot eight steers and left them lying. They had just started to sweeten the air. They were one and all Durham halfbreeds, wearing the Enterprise 44 brand. Not a pretty sight. It is considered a crime of the worst order to shoot cattle on the range, and is more generally condemned than shooting people. Such a waste, and they can't protect themselves. At least with people you can always hope they did something to deserve it.

I rode from one to the next. They had been shot through apparently with a gun of large calibre. It was just the wound which would come from Ma's old Sharps. They were on our range where they had no business being, so I couldn't but think she had been driven to such action as a last resort when they tried to take over—but still it sickened me. This was going too far. But then I thought, wait, maybe she *didn't* do it. Maybe this is exactly what they wanted people to believe, that she'd done it.

I rode on and didn't look back. I rode straight in line with the creek, staying clear by a couple of miles. Dark settled as I rode, a thick and heavy twilight, the sort one gets when it's toward autumn, with the longer nights. Came to an old lake bed. It was all curled gumbo dry and crunching under the hoofs. There was

179

brush marking the creek. All heavy and dark. The moon came up, huge in size but not bright. The bigger your moon the less light it gives. I let Old Keno go as he wished, and he went down to water. We both drank our fill. The mosquitoes were singing, but it was hard for them to find you in the dark, though late mosquitoes are generally the fiercest of the year. There was a slight breeze, or rather a drift of air, and we went with it, up the valley, and they lost us. In the dark always ride with the wind, not against it, when trying to lose your mosquito.

Could hear the rustling of prairie chickens under the bullberries. They clucked in the dark. Avoided them, not wanting to put them in flight. Drumming wings give the secret traveler away. Came to a place where trees filled the valley solid. These were mainly box-elders, a few cottonwoods. Absolutely black. I couldn't see a thing. Let Old Keno take me on slack rein. Had to watch out for branches. He'd walk under things with bare room for him, no thought to the rider. One of those big box-elder limbs could scrape you right off. And any stray bullberry twig became like unto that new hellish invention, the barbed wire.

The brush fell away, and we were in a little park where cattle liked to bed down in the heat of day. Their smells were around. Yet he balked, refused to go another foot. I had to get off and lead. "Come on, dang ye!" and I backed against something solid and heavy.

Gad! it sent a shock through me. It was a dead body. I almost dropped the bridle and ran. If so I'd have lost everything. I'd never have found my way back. I stood stock still, clutching the bridle whilst shudders coursed up and down my body. I shook in every muscle, and my teeth chattered. But it passed. I became absolutely calm.

"Well, let's see what we got," says I.

I groped and found it. I took right hold of it. It had hung there long enough to go absolutely solid. The legs had been tied together. I let go and it swung back and forth and the limb dipped, creaked. The limb had bent until his boots almost touched the ground. The grass and weeds rustled. Thought he never would stop swinging. He was heavy as a side of beef. Dead weight is far heavier than live weight.

Naturally I was scared it was Rusty. So far I hadn't seen a thing. Only the slight movement of limb and leaves against the sky. I had to make sure. There was no way except by striking a match. A risk that had to be taken. I did it—how bright the flame seemed!—but still I couldn't tell who it was. He was all pulled out of shape and his head was lopped away over, gorged and terrible. I held the match, and held it, and noticed that his belt buckle was one of the kind made by Navajo Indians out of a Mexican peso. It was the Ringbone Kid!

I'll own to being relieved, and to not liking him very much. I guess you could say I was scared of him. You'd make a friendly remark and he'd scoff as if you weren't very bright. Now all was of the past. I was struck by how he was simply an object, just a hunk of meat. Sounds terrible, but that's how I felt. Here was an argument for the Preacher to use on Rusty and all his atheist talk, because there was not the slightest doubt that the real essence of Ringbone had departed. In other words, the soul.

Ka-whack! I was startled from my reverie by a gunshot, and *wak-wak-wak!* echoes bounding off the cutbanks. Then *ki-yi-yi!* the coyotes got into it.

They weren't shooting at me. It was quite a ways off. You'd hear what seemed to be a high-speed rifle, and then a deeper sound, a *ka-woom!* which was probably the Sharps. Counted about twenty shots. Slow and careful I moved on up the creek.

Dismounted. Tied Old Keno to a drag so he could get feed and water in case I was shot, captured. Yet I felt no fear. Went on afoot with six shooter, rifle, cartridge belt over shoulder, also cartridges in pockets. All were .44 calibre, fitting both guns. Could see no powder flashes because of the trees and the sheds, but the smell came, powder, and as if an old quilt had been set afire.

I reached the sheds. They were of poles, unchinked and you could see right through them; you could watch the house unseen if it had been light; they made shelter for cattle, from sun and storm, and were a small protection from stray bullets, but they posed a danger, too, being of quaking asp poles which, dry and hard, flew to jagged slivers if hit.

I got to a roof and lay for a while. They were shooting from the old house, and also from a dry channel under a cutbank, I couldn't figure what they were shooting at. Then *whoom!* a much heavier calibre, a regular old cannon. I realized then that Ma had taken refuge in the root cellar. It was the only answer.

Most root cellars are mere holes in the ground, deep enough to keep potatoes from freezing in our fifty degrees of winter cold. Not Stamp's. He'd dug it back into a reef, or hill, that rose from the creek bottom. It boasted wooden steps, and sides lines with poles. There was a pole roof with a layer of shale and sod.

The sod didn't green much, but weeds had taken root and grew up every summer, and there was a ventilator. The door was double plank with layers of gunny sack, etc., to keep out the cold.

Whoom! that old cannon went every so often, but no powder trail to be seen. Indeed the root cellar was her refuge!

Chapter Nineteen

"Gods and fiends" exclaimed the wounded knight; "Oh for one moment's strength, to drag myself into the melee, and perish as becomes my name"

—*Ivanhoe*

I set out for Ma's fortress, keeping to the steep side of the reef. This topographical feature was a hundred yards long and bare of bushes except where gullies cut in, and there you found some buckbrush, squaw currant, sage and the like. Men were out and about under the stars, talking and laughing, even smoking cigarettes, just careful not to show themselves out in front of that root cellar door where Ma would blast them to kingdom come.

What I wanted was to get close enough to talk to her, let her know she wasn't alone in the world. Wanted to let her know Rusty and I hadn't been hung. Also learn the truth of what was happening; who had shot the steers? Were the General and Hoffner leagued against her? And in the back of my mind was the hope I'd be able to stage a diversion and rescue her. I might even, if it got dark enough, pull some of the sod and poles off the roof and effect her escape—though hoisting that big, heavy woman without block and tackle *would* pose quite a problem!

With these thoughts I prowled along, seeking what cover I could. Moon up full, big as a dish pan. Could hear men talking but chiefly the *tones* of their voices, their cuss-words, little of what was actually said. Somebody would laugh and remark, and there was a lot of filthy talk. A low-life bunch if there ever was one. They were typical of the dregs which enlist on the side of money and power no matter how sorry the cause.

A lot of their talk was about Ma, and I wouldn't put it down. Then somebody said they were supposed to go someplace, to such and such a position, and a fellow said damned if he would. "Let *him* go!" "You want me to carry that message?" And they wrangled for a while. Then they must have had each a drink of whisky because I could smell it, a pungent barb on the night air.

I waited, wanting to see what they were going to do. They had some plan or other but none of them wanted to be first and take a chance.

"Mrs. Irons, do you hear me?" a man yelled. "Mrs. Irons!"

"Yes!" Her voice came muffled, and if you hadn't known you'd never have guessed from what direction. "I hear you."

"I want to talk to you."

"Well, you're *talkin'*."

"A truce, Mrs. Irons. We have no want to harm you."

"You'll get no truce from me!" Then she says, "You better get me soon because I got help comin'."

"No, you haven't. Your sons have left the country." Long pause. "They skedaddled, Mrs. Irons!" As if we and not them were the cowards! "We hung one of their badlanders!" There must have been discussion about this because he said, "We hung one and shot another. There's nobody left."

I knew who they'd hung, but not who they'd shot, but I did recall seeing the two horses with empty saddles. This went on for quite a time. Couldn't recognize the voice. Suspected it was Casey Hobbs, our new sheriff.

"I have to arrest you for shooting cattle. That's my sworn duty, and Monte would have done the same." She must have said something because he said, "Whether they're estray or not, you can't shoot them, and that's the law."

It must have been she came up the steps because her voice was suddenly loud and clear. "Get off my property. You're in trespass and that's the law, too."

"I have a warrant, Thelma."

"Don't you *Thelma* me. You treat me with respect. I'm Mrs. Irons to you."

"Well, Mrs. Irons, I'm here to serve a warrant and I'm giving you this final chance."

She stopped heeding him. She kept muttering and ejaculating, and he said, "Mrs. Irons, I'm here to declare a truce." Then he must have talked to somebody, I could hear other voices, and he said, "Look at me! I'm unarmed. Unarmed I'm coming to talk to you."

This roused her again and she said, "Stay where you are because I don't like shooting an unarmed man. It's a trick, anyhow. You got no honor. You're a lackey for the corporations. You're in cahoots." And she went on about how if he ran for his office, instead of getting it handed to him by appointment, there weren't twenty people in the county that would vote for him. "You're in league with evil! You're in league with the devil." It started her in on Scripture. "Yea, ye and your minions of Gehenna, driving widows out of their homes. Ye will be damned! Ye shall be consumed by the everlasting fire," etc.

Then, *ka-boom!* she took another shot with the old Sharps. They'd come out to listen, but oh! did they scramble for cover!

"You are devils! You have the mark of the beast!" She wasn't underground any more. She was yelling right out at them. She had to have the door opened, of course, or she couldn't have shot. She couldn't have *breathed*, closed in with that old smokehouse of a gun. "You have worshiped the beast! Yea, you have received the mark of *the beast* upon your foreheads. You shall drink of the wine of the wrath of God. So is it written in the books of these latter days. And you shall be tormented with fire and brimstone in the presence of The Lamb!"

"She says we're sheepherders!" some jackanapes yelled, but she went on unheeding—

"God will smite you for your iniquities! There shall be a plague upon nations, and death, and mourning, and famine, and the whole world shall be visited by a plague of grasshoppers, and they shall be as fiery brass, and their stings shall be as the stings of scorpions and serpents!"

They started to whoop and taunt. "You hear that? We're going to get stung by red-hot grasshoppers!"

". . . And the smoke of torment shall rise forever, and they shall rest neither by day nor by night. And behold! An angel sat on a cloud, and the angel cried out, 'Thrust in thy sickle and reap, for the harvest of the earth is ripe, and the grapes would be picked, but the wine would be blood.' " It was really frightening.

She sounded much like Preacher Harlow when he got to going at Rusty. Then she got to the part about Babylon.

"Aye, Babylon is fallen, is fallen. Go thy ways O Babylon and pour thy vials of wrath upon the earth. And this shall be the first judgment. Babylon is fallen, is fallen! It has become the habitation of devils and the hold of every foul spirit and cage of every hateful and unclean bird, for all the nations have drunk of the wrath of her fornication, and the kings of the earth likewise, and the merchants have waxed rich through the abundance of her luxuries, but her sins have reached to heaven, and she *shall* be visited by grasshoppers whose bodies are of brass, and their stings are of the fiery scorpion! It shall come to pass! This is the word of God, do you hear that, ye devils who come here and torture a poor widow in the name of the beast?"

They were listening in spite of themselves. When Ma got all fired and going it was enough to give anybody pause, no matter how hard-case he claimed to be. It used to drive Pa right out of the house.

"The great Whore of Babylon!" she got to yelling. "You are all minions of that *Great Whore,* who is the perfumed beast of wickedness. For she hath the breath of corruption and the hair of serpents, and the serpents are of brass, but the cup in her hand is the cup of gold. You hear that, you wolves?"

They heard her! They naturally listened when she got to talking about a whore, because whores were right in their line. It was what they chiefly talked about when at their ease.

"She's talkin' about Katie Maxwell!" one of them whooped. "Katie must be coming up in the world!"

Katie was the madame in at Steele I told about in

Chapter X. It might have seemed like a funny remark, but none of them were laughing. The scene was too dark and terrible.

"Ye shall descend into the bottomless pit!" cried Ma, going straight on, because nothing could give her pause once the power of the Word came over her. "Ye shall be cast into the everlasting fire. And all your kind will wax in perdition. And the people, and the multitudes, and the nations, and the tongues, so shall they also. And all shall loathe thee, and ye shall be made desolate and naked, all ye who consort with the Great Whore, ye shall eat her flesh and burn her with fire, all ye who have drunk of the wine of her fornications, yea, even the kings of the earth who have committed fornications with her, and the merchants of the earth, and all who have worshiped the calf of gold."

When Ma said Babylon she meant Fort Steele. I know this because I've heard her on the subject before, and not long before, either, but when she came home after being turned down at the bank.

"Alas, that great city! In a single hour will her judgment come! And nobody will buy her merchandise. And silver and gold and fine linen. Yea, Babylon is fallen, is fallen! It has become the habitation of devils. And the hold of every unclean bird. For the nation hath drunk the wine of her fornications. Ye shall be cast down. Ye shall scream in the lakes of everlasting fire . . ."

Ere this they resumed their shooting. I don't imagine she was pleasant to listen to. There's hardly anybody who doesn't have *some* fear of an afterlife in his bones, and to hear somebody who actually *believes*, well, it gives him a disquiet. And Ma believed. She just had *no doubt at all.*

There was nothing for them to aim at except the top part of the root cellar. *Whop!* you could hear their bullets. You could smell the busted wood, and the earth, and what must have been old sacking put in to keep out the cold. Nothing took fire, but could you see the flame! This often happened with an old, loose barrel gun. The rifling may be shot out and the bullet takes a lot of burning powder with it. The main purpose they had, if they'd thought it out, could only be to shoot the top part of the old root cellar to pieces and bring it down atop of her, her refuge becoming her grave. But of course they *hadn't* thought it out. They just kept blasting away because there was nothing else for them to do, and the ammunition was free, being paid for by our tax money.

Finally it slackened off. The guns were getting hot to the touch, no doubt. I could hear men talking nearby. I crept along, watching out for poison oak. By day this can be recognized because it turns red sooner than any other plant, but all colors are gray in the moonlight. I stayed in the buckbrush where possible. Buckbrush gets its name from buck deer liking to hide in it. Even with heads up and eyes watching you can't see them—it blends so even with their antlers. There was considerable of this, but at last I had to come into the open.

"Better not go up there, soldier!"

I'd come right up to a fellow without noticing. He had been standing there still, and it's movement you notice. I didn't know his voice, hence he wouldn't know mine.

"Why not?"

"You get to stirring around on top and she'll hear you. She'll blast you from below."

"I'm going to scout it anyhow."

"Go ahead, it's your funeral."

I moved on, still finding cover where possible. Next man might not be a stranger. I could hear them talking one place and another, and smell whisky being passed about. Had to be careful when I got on top for fear they'd start shooting again. Crawled the last few yards. The roof was covered with about two feet of dirt, as I said. The only way of telling where the reef ended and the roof began was by the weeds which were different from elsewhere. They were mainly tall mustard, one of our so-called tumbleweeds. These were called "one-legged tumbleweeds" because of how they would leap as they rolled along, similar to a wooden-legged man running.

Turned out they were grown over quite an area. I edged through and heard a hollow sound, so I was there! Stopped in a hurry let me tell you! What a cruel trick of fate if she heard me and shot upwards, killing her own son!

Looked for the ventilator. Well concealed amidst the mustard. It was made of four boards, forming a pipe, and was fitted with a shake to keep out rain. It descended all the way through the root cellar with its opening no more than six inches from the floor. This way it carried out all cold air and damp which tended to settle.

"Ma?" says I, *sotto voce*, lips close to the opening.

She didn't hear me. Listened with one ear, heard her muttering and moving about. A smell arose of heat and burning, and human smell. It must have been fearsome dense down there. She was talking to herself, or to Pa. "No, I'll not relinquish an inch! I won't give 'em a hair. This is ours to have and to keep. I gave my solemn promise."

191

"Ma!" I said louder, where the warm smell rose.
She stopped. I could *feel* her listening.

"Ma?"

"Who's there?" she asked, shaken.

"It's me, Hank."

"Henry?"

"Yes."

"Oh, dear God. What are you doing down there?
Oh, God, they killed you and you're in the nether re-
gions."

This left me baffled. Then I realized my voice came
out by her feet, where the ventilator opened. She
thought I was in the depths. She thought they'd killed
me and I'd gone to hell!

"Ma, I'm up here."

"Oh, Henry, Henry! Make yourself manifest!"

"I'm *alive*. I'm on the roof talking down the ventilator."

"What?"

"I said I was talking down the air hole."

She stood there and stood there. I could feel the stillness of her, and her listening, her caution and suspicion because she thought it all might be a trick of the
devil.

"Ma? Listen to me. I'm alive. They never killed me.
Didn't hang me, nor Rusty. He's away and safe. I
come home. I follered you here. They hung Ringbone
and killed Preacher, maybe, but I'm all right. Ma, we
got to get away."

"If they see you they'll shoot you. Why, you must
be *in plain view!*"

"It's dark. It's near midnight."

"Oh. Well, *keep down!* Crawl around here by the
cutbank side."

"No, we got to get out and away."

192

"You're talking wild. There's no way I can get out. They'll pelt me a thousand screed." She seemed sort of out of her head. "I'm all shot up. I think they put out my nether eye. I'm all cut by splinters. One went right through my arm and broke off. Oh, what have I done to deserve this suffering?"

"Ma! You got to get out of there."

"Oh, foolish talk! You're the one that better get out and away. I'll keep 'em shot down whilst you run for it."

"No, I don't need any help up here. I can get away. I'll surprise them and you make a run for it."

She said it was tomfool talk, and who did I think I was, Buffalo Bill Cody? And I said no, but I had men backing me. She didn't believe it, of course, she'd listened to *big talk* all her life, and she said, "Oh, yes, big talk, big talk! Who could you have backing you? The whole country is down on us."

"I got my badlanders."

"You have not. You're lying. You got nobody."

"Come out and have a look!"

"Save yourself. Skedaddle!"

"I ain't going to. We're leaving together."

"Oh, stubborn, stubborn! Bullheaded and stubborn."

"Ma, I'm going to raise a big whoop and start shooting. That'll be a signal for you to come out. Head for the cutbank side."

"Stubborn," she kept muttering, "stubborn."

I had to hope she'd make a run for it and I could cause a diversion so they wouldn't shoot her down. It was a chance, though a long one.

I moved back the way I'd come, more difficult going down than up. Did it feet first, dragging rifle, pistol, etc.

"Hey!" I had crawled almost atop somebody. It was the same man I'd talked to before. "Who are you, anyhow?" he asked.

"Homer Clinchhammer." People will always accept a peculiar name over a common one. Had I said I was Bill Brown he wouldn't have believed me for a second.

"What's wrong?" asked he.

"The badlanders are coming, about twenty strong. They got a Gatling gun."

This was a mistake. It gave him too much to think about.

"Where'd they get a Gatling gun?"

"How do I know? They stole it from the Army, I suppose."

"Hey, Wally," he called out. "You know what Clinchhammer tells me? The badlanders are coming and they got a Gatling gun."

"Who tells you this?" This big fellow—he looked like a great bear, hunched and peering—came up the slope trying to make me out. "What'd you say your name was?"

I could see it was up with me, so I said, "Clinchhammer!" and poked the rifle at him. You're always better with a rifle than a pistol, even at close quarters. You can use it like a thrust, and you got fifteen shots in the magazine, not six.

He didn't see it and came prowling forward and *whang!* I got a shot off. I hadn't intended to, any more than at Skinner. But one can't call it pure accident. It said something about my nature. I suppose it was the Irons in me.

He spun around and almost fell. "Ow! ow!" he yelled. Then he fell and went thrashing around, yelling, "Ow! Christ, Jesus, I been hit!"

I'd shot into the ground, actually, just in front of his feet, only the bullet must have glanced, because the next thing he got to yelling was, "Ow! my leg's broke. I can't walk." And, "Ow, ow, ow! my boot is full of blood."

Accident or not, I was quick to see he was the best thing I had going for me.

"Ya-hoo!" I yelled, the time-honored cry of the raider and shot some more. "We're coming out of the badlands!" I yelled.

Gad, did they light out from there! They didn't stop to help that wounded fellow *at all!* They were a-scramble to save their own hides, let the devil take the hindmost. It proved what a craven bunch they were, typical of the kind that hang out in towns and enlist in posses, out to kill at no risk, and carve out a braggard's reputation.

Shot the rifle empty and turned to the pistol. After six shots with the pistol my hand was absolutely numb. I tried to reload and couldn't even feel the cartridges. Got them out of my pocket and spilled them on the ground. Had trouble finding them. All this took time. It is much easier to feed cartridges into a rifle than a pistol. I was at this in a dogged manner when *zing!* a bullet tore the ground from under my boots.

"Hold your ground!" yelled Casey Hobbs. "I'll kill the first man that runs."

Getting ready to meet the badlanders attack, you see! I'd fooled him if only briefly. Then *Boom!* went the old Sharps, the loudest I'd heard it. She must have been up on the dugout steps.

"Ma!" I yelled. "Ma, I'm up here."

She didn't answer, so I ran that way, caution cast aside. Next thing I knew I was flat on the ground. It was as if I'd been hit by a club. I didn't pass out. I was aware all the while, but time was scaled in a new way. It seemed to hang around me. I tried to get up and the ground slid away. It was like standing on a blanket and somebody pulls it ever so slow. I had to get down on my hands and knees, and even then I rolled over. It took me a while to realize it was from the steepness. I'd been hit by a glancing bullet. My head seemed to be partly carried off. I felt it with both hands. My head was all there, I could feel *it* but *it* couldn't feel me, a very strange sensation. I'd never known anything more baffling. I took my hat off and put it on again, but there was absolutely no sensation of it being on my head. My rifle and pistol were gone. I felt all along the ground. I was naked unto my enemies.

Whoom! I heard that Sharps go once more. And *Whoom!* again, fast as she could feed cartridges into it. It was a single-shot. Then I saw her. What I recall seeing was an *apparition* of Ma. It might have been the state I was in, knocked unsteady by whatever had hit me. This ghostly thing rose from the root cellar. It seemed to ascend the steps and float. I thought they had killed her. I thought her body was left behind and her spirit was ascending on its final earthly journey.

Actually what I saw was not so much Ma as her big, Mother Hubbard dress. She made these herself out of Dauntless Bleach cotton, a light gray sheeting she bought by the bolt. It cost 4 cents per yard and she sewed them of large size for comfort and to keep off the dust while driving.

A man rose up right in front of her. He'd crawled up close to get a good shot, and there she was, pointblank range.

"Ma!" I yelled to warn her. I don't whether a sound

passed my lips. All was off-center and in a float on account of the blow I'd taken. No warning was necessary. She had that old buffalo gun waist-high. *Kaboom!* and she simply blew him out of the way.

"Halt! Halt!" said Casey Hobbs, coming forth from the house. "You are under arrest."

He certainly had his nerve, I'll say that for him. He was taking his sheriff's office seriously. An evil man and a bully, but he didn't hide from what could be described as a juggernaut.

"Drop that rifle, Mrs. Irons!"

He pulled down on her. He had a rifle and aimed from the shoulder. He aimed it so long I could see the moonlight play on its barrel, an octagonal barrel, $2.50 exra. He might have thought he was safe because Ma was shooting a single-shot gun. Why, that woman could load in her sleep! She could have done it one-handed whilst churning cream. Both of them fired. I could see the twin flames rushing to meet. Less than a dozen strides separated them. Both could have fallen. But it was not to be. Fate had taken a hand in this deadly play and decreed that Ma's bullet was as a hair's-breadth of time sooner. It lifted Casey right back over his heels, while his bullet flew high. It mighty near hit *me*. I could hear it *hum-m!* the wind of it; had the feeling I could have reached back and plucked it from the air. Casey hit the ground so hard it knocked his hat off. He lay flat with arms outflung. The life had been smashed out of him. For self-protection there is no gun equal to the old Buffalo Sharps!

Soon men came from everywhere. I hadn't realized there were so many. Some were in flight and some wanted to get a shot in. Ma killed Ed Peale, the famed pistoleer of the Indian Territories. I didn't actually see

197

this happen, but his body was identified. "Mr. Peale was unarmed when found," read the account in the Miles City paper, as if she had taken unfair advantage of a man who carried twelve notches on his gun. They robbed him of all his valuables, and turned his pockets inside out, but "unarmed" got in the paper. Not a word against his ghoulish friends. Also she killed Jack Whitaker and a shifty little poolroom skite they called "Ace in the Hole." This worthy had been shot in the back, according to reports. He was high-tailing it out of there, of course, and Tom Ward, or somebody, figured he wasn't getting a full degree of loyalty. It saddens me to note that Long Henry Carmichael was wounded, to die two weeks later in Dr. McCleary's hospital at Steele. He was a no-good hoot, but friendly.

Back to the scene of smoke and carnage. I passed out for a time and then I noticed that Ma was nowhere about. I looked all over the ground, from my vantage point expecting to see her body. Not so. She had walked away, just walked, no hurry, and had got to the corrals. These were about an eighth of a mile above the house. And there she was, hitching her buggy! The horses had been uncoupled and put to graze; they must have had their harness dragging, because all she had to do it seemed, was fasten the tugs to the rings. Took her time, didn't try to stay out of view, nothing. And nobody bothered her. Believe me, they'd had all they wanted of *her*. Then I saw the Brigadier! It was as if everything was coupled up, or foreshortened, like seeing things through a telescope. Not a vision. He was there, mounted on one of his fine bays. He sat ramrod stiff and she rode straight past. He could have shot her down with even a derringer.

He could have killed her with a rock! Or, if that had lowered him in class, he could have ordered Tom Ward to do it. But he just sat there and watched her drive away! All slow, as in a dream.

Chapter Twenty

He gave his bridle reins a shake,
Said, "Adieu for evermore."

—*Rokeby*

". . . as in a dream." I can't to this hour recall finding my horse, but I was astraddle him, good old Keno. The sun shone hard against my eyeballs. Night had passed. My head was numb no longer, it pained and throbbed. The side of my head felt like a single large and painful lump. I couldn't see what my wound looked like, of course. I was hardly able to feel whether I'd been creased, or shot through with the bullet inside, or whether I'd been clouted by a rock. There was a hole in my hat. The looks of this, big and ragged, and some bloody hair which came from my scalp, led me to believe I had taken what was known as a flat glance, i.e. a bullet which bounces off sidewise to the rifling.

Keno stopped to drink and I had some, too. It was a pothole, warm and muddy. I drank and drank, and lay for a long time after. Keno went off to graze, but I managed to catch him. Mounting to the saddle took all the strength I had. I hung on belly-over to the mane for a while. What was known as the sack of oats style. I had heard of people who slept that way whilst riding, but it didn't work for me. Dreamed I'd found my guns.

Not so. All I had were pockets full of bullets. I'd lost revolver and rifle, both. I was unarmed, I rode wherever Keno wanted to take me. That night I was at the Madlow Buttes. I slept there, if it could be called sleeping. I spent the black hours beset by the wildest of visions. When it came light Keno was gone. I didn't have a drop of water. I suffered torments of thirst. The nearest water I knew about was Cottonwood Creek, so I set off afoot, in my busted boots, up one coulee side and down another, across the grain of the country.

I hadn't eaten, and this added to my problem. Hunger didn't bother, but I was weak. I had to stop every few hundred steps and set my mind to keep from wandering. I had to tighten my belt to the last hole, one I'd left behind two years before, but partly this was due to the weight of the cartridges in my pockets. I had no gun yet could not bring myself to throw them away.

I walked and when too tired to go on I rested. I was there, looking back, when I saw something move— and it was Old Keno! I thought first it was a vision, but no, there he was! He had been follering me.

I got up to catch him, but this he would not let me do. I set out once more. Every time I walked, he walked, and keeping much the same distance. So it went through the hours, and at last I got to Uncle Will's, and there, at the edge of pasture, he let me get on. I was thankful for even one mile. I was back on Wildhorse water. There is none better in all the land. Sandstone springs, no iron, no soda. I drank and drank. I actually lay in the creek, taking in its cool wetness through the skin, and when revived I went to the house, built a fire and cooked some doughgods of flour there in a can, made tea, and fell down on the bed. Slept like a side of beef.

When I woke up it was dark and the wolves were

howling. These were wolves, not coyotes. They liked that rough country of which Cottonwood Creek was a part. I'd never heard them howl like that. Uncle Will trapped, shot or poisoned 167 wolves his first season on the homestead, and this sounded like the olden days. What had set them off? *Ow-ow-owoooo!*

After listening for what seemed like an hour I got up in my naked feet, went outside on the hard grass, and looked toward a ruddy light in the sky. It was where our ranch was. Either that had set them off, or there'd been shooting. I figured the gang had burnt us out.

Went back to bed. I wasn't much scared they'd be here next, I was too bone tired. The main thing was to get my head in a position that didn't hurt. I slept and woke up somewhat startled by a memory of what by then seemed to have been a dream—wolves, ruddy glow of fire, etc. Whether dream or no, I knew they would come for Ma for all the shooting. You can't shoot a sheriff, no matter what a skunk he is. So I rode home, very cautious the final half mile . . .

The ranch lay absolutely still. The barns and sheds all there—bunkhouse and cookhouse, Rusty's place, etc., but something was missing. Well, there I sat looking, and it was the house! It wasn't there! There was a little, shrunken place where a fire had been, a bedstead, the stove with pipe attached, charred timbers, and the sill logs, but the area they squared off was too small. Yet there was the path leading to it, Ma's flower patch, the tub and chopping block. And there stood the chimney, solid clay brick. Was this where we'd spent the good times and hard, and the long nights with Ma reading by the light of the lamp? Finally she'd close the book and say, "That's all for to-night. Why, come to gracious, it must be ten o'clock."

A dead hen lay with her feet sticking out. A vagrant

breeze turned her feathers. More hens, all shot. They'd had target practice. All else perfectly quiet. Many tracks about and horse manure some hours old.

I went back and turned my horse into the corral. Left him saddled so I could get away in a hurry. Came back, still wary, watching for any kind of sign. "Hey!" I called, not too loud. "Hey, who's about?"

Something got to moving about; I took it first to be a bear. No, I thought, not a bear, it's a huge, shaggy dog. It took on human shape and turned out to be Dad Marsh, crawling from under the cache house, absolutely covered with dirt and litter.

"Dad!" I called, but got there in a hurry, because he had his old needle gun, and up to his shoulder it came.

"Dad, it's me! Hank!"

He stood with that rifle raised for the longest time, but finally it got through to him.

"Oh, Hank!" It was as if he hadn't heard of me for years, and the memory had to work through. His eyes looked a bit crazy, but I took a chance and walked toward him. He peered all around and shook some of the dirt off, hay and leaves and old hen manure, and I don't know what all. "They didn't kill you, huh?"

I didn't want to start that again. "Of course not. I'm here, ain't I? I ain't been hung or shot or nothing."

He kept staring at me. He didn't seem to be able to get things into his mind.

"What happened to Ma?" I asked.

"They took her away."

"Arrested her?"

"Why would they do that? She burnt up in the house."

Truly I hadn't expected this. It left me wobbly.

"They waited for it to cool off and then they went in

and kicked around, and found what of her hadn't burned, and they put it in a sack and hauled it out to the old turnip patch and buried it. Then they rode back and forth over the place so's you wouldn't be able to tell, just like they used to drive wagons over the graves so the Indians couldn't take scalp in the olden days. I lay right here and watched 'em. I saw every bit from the hay shed. They had no idea I was there or they'd have burnt me out, too. Are you all right?"

"Yes, I'm all right!" I said, shaking off his hands. Never could endure having old people feel of me.

"What you need is a drink of whisky!"

He went to where a bottle was hid. It was a quart with only about one third gone. It wasn't his own. I knew by how he looked at the label. Ma never allowed whisky on the premises.

"They hid this and couldn't find it again. Fellow named Boltner hid it, and they looked all over. I knew where it was, though."

He wiped some of the litter off his moustache and had a big snort, shaking himself after like a dog coming from water.

"They had to keep this out of McKibbin's sight. Oh, they was sober! They couldn't use that as an excuse."

"McKibbin was along, then?"

"Of course he was. Oh, he was the big *general!* He was old U.S. Grant taking Vicksburg!"

"Give me that bottle!" I said. "I may have a swig of it after all!"

I can't say the liquor helped my head any. Every time I moved at all quick the dizziness came back. It was still so puffed my hat wouldn't sit. Dad wouldn't stop talking. He had to tell me everything twice over. I went and lay down by the spring. I pulled up moss and mint and laid it over my head. After half an hour I felt able to finish my look around, and even go poke through the house. A lot of dishes and hardware could be picked up, and the brass bindings of Pa's record books.

"Did McKibbin stand by for this?"

"They went wild, searching the place. They turned everything upside down, searching for Rusty. 'Bring any mail you find to me,' he said. They brought him a lot of old letters and stuff. He just kind of sneered at it and tossed it away. He didn't care what they did. They looted and busted things in general. They had an egg fight."

I could see where eggs had been smashed.

"Exactly when was this?"

"Yesterday."

"Where was Ma?"

"In the house. She wouldn't come out. She had come in driving the rig. I tried to talk to her, wanted to help, but she went to the house and closed the door. She wasn't nowhere near herself. It was as if she knew they were coming after her, and was getting ready to meet her fate."

Dad was right. She could guess what lay in store for her.

"Did the General ride up at the head of his troops?"

"No, they came a few at a time. I see the first of 'em lurking around the pastures and the corrals. They came in closer and skulking, and I hid out. I wanted to hear what they had plans to do. I heard they'd been attacked by a gang of badlanders over at the Stamp place, and Ma had shot somebody down in cold blood."

"*Somebody?* Oh, cripes!"

"That's what they said, shot him *in cold blood!* They said they'd made the mistake of going easy on her because she was an old lady, but now they were in no mood to show mercy. I knew a couple of them. They had eaten right at our table. Mostly they were from down in Texas, New Mexico. You can tell by how they talk. That fellow that used to play the fiddle and had a shack out at Tiger Butte, he was along. Then Whip Cotton come and ordered them all down behind the sheds. It was on account of General McKibbin. Didn't want anybody lost. Oh, was he runnin' things! He rode up like Almighty God and looked at everything through his spyglass. The reason I could see was I crawled up where the hay was stacked in the new shed. I got to where I wasn't more than two feet from the roof. It got dreadful hot, but I was able to see, and that was the important thing. McKibbin was all decked out in his cavalry gear like when he led the parade on July Fourth. He had all but his sword. He had on his campaign hat."

I took this with a grain of salt. I didn't figure he'd gone home and changed.

"After the General arrived there was some order to things and they searched the place. They went over it like they had a harrow. I crawled deep down in the hay and they waded through, and they poked with pitchforks, but never found me. I had wanted to crawl under the floor, down under the old storehouse, where Tippy had her pups, but they looked there, and when they couldn't see anything they went around shooting through the floor 'Come out!' they yelled. 'Come out, we know you're down there!' but I don't think they were looking for me. They were looking for Rusty. But I could see they didn't expect to find him. They were doing it all for the General, but he just sat back by the spring and smoked cigars. He watched to make sure nobody rode away from the pasture, or from the house. He watched the house all the time.

"Well, he rode off with Ward and the gang got to tearing things up. They were completely lawless. They got to shooting the chickens. McKibbin wasn't so far but what he knew what was happening. He has to take the blame. He thought killing the chickens might get Ma to come out. I could see the shine of his glass. They would run a hen down on horseback and toss her in the air, and *bang!* they would all shoot at her. Cotton didn't like it. He was the only one with the least decency about him. He finally put a stop to it and went up and tried to talk to Ma. He was taking his life in his hands, the way she'd become, sort of crazy. And of course she actually slept with that gun. Yes, Hank, she did! She took it right to bed beside her.

" 'Let us search the house and if your son isn't there we'll be on our way,' he said. He had an old tin can cut out to use as a voice magnifier. Finally he gave up and rode back to talk with the General, and then he came and talked with Tom Ward, and Tom Ward came over and says to somebody that they'd have to smoke her out, it was the only way, because she probably had enough food and water to last a month. Then it got dark, and I heard McKibbin hisself; he came right down here and wasn't more'n ten feet away.

" 'I'll go talk to her,' he says.

" 'She'll shoot you. That old woman's not right in the head.'

" 'She didn't shoot you, did she?'

"Besides, it was too dark to see much. Couldn't aim. Anyhow, up there he went. He got off and walked to the gate. I could hear him saying, 'Thelma!' Called her by her own name. 'This is Otis. Otis McKibbin.' "

" 'Get off my ranch!' your ma yelled.

"He said a lot more and so did she, but I had a hard time hearing. The dust got in on me something fierce. Howsomever, I did hear him say, 'Mrs. Irons, I'll give you ten minutes and no longer!' Oh, everybody heard that! He said it good and loud so they would would bear witness! 'Ten minutes,' he says, 'after which we shall feel free to enter that house one means or another!'

"They *might* have waited ten minutes. It didn't seem so to me. Pretty soon there was shooting, and Cotton went around warning them they was to aim high, through the upper part of the house, shoot the roof first, but I don't know, so far as I could see they did as they pleased. In fact they just settled in and cut that house to flinders."

"Did Ma do any shooting?"

"Early she did, but not later on. Not as I could tell. There was so much racket and she was so far off. They shot, and they shot. They shot till their guns were fouled and you could see the live coals fly for a hundred yards. It was only a question of time before they set the house on fire, it's been so dry. You could smell stuff burning for a long time. It must have smoldered for hours. I even dozed for a time. There was a lot of smoke finally, but no flame. It got so you could see the red glow through the near window.

" 'Watch for them when they come out,' the Brigadier said. He said 'them' so he still must have believed Rusty was there. Rusty was the one he'd come after. Every bad thing that happened to this ranch has been on account of your brother—"

"Never mind," says I.

"Then there was a big *whoof!* and of a sudden the house was *all aflame!* It busted through the roof, just like a banked fire in a stove when it explodes."

He wanted to tell a lot more, but I didn't want to listen. He told about the smells of burnt flesh, etc., and he had a long-winded account of Ma rising above the flames. She *ascended* and he could hear her yelling, "Pa, Pa, I'm a-coming!" But I didn't believe him, I figured she'd got killed early or she'd have bagged some of 'em like she had at Stamp's. And he had to tell over and over in detail how they gathered and buried her remains. All in all not the thing a son likes to listen to.

Chapter Twenty-one

"Farewell, sweet homey lands, we ride at last into the maw of hell, land most parched and terrible."
—Ivanhoe

D ad found enough food for a breakfast, which I ate with good appetite, despite all. I walked around and surveyed the damage done, picked up a few mementos, arrowheads and the like; they had taken the Damascus shotgun, which was mine, and all else easily lifted and salable. Rusty's papers and books were scattered. They'd torn his Hiawatha down the middle. It was wanton. But I spent little time on exprobations (blame), useless at all events.

"They're just likely to come back," I remarked. "We better shag out of here, *muy pronto.*"

Dad went pale at these words. It was his home, you see, and it came to him as a fact that he'd have to leave for good, to set forth into the uncertain world. It gets that way with the old; they're scareder of moving than they are of dying.

"We're coming back, ain't we?"

I didn't have the heart to tell him it was doubtful;

that he was looking at the last of the Ironses. "It'll be a while. You better take your valuables."

They'd run off all the horses, and I needed a mount for him, and who should come moseying up from the creek but Old Hazel, the mare which you may recall from my journey to the Hole in the Wall. She had gone lame-footed some time after this, and Ardis had pulled the shoes off her, but she'd hung around, and I was able to catch her.

"Where are we going?" asked Dad. "Why, the whole country will be set against us."

"They don't love McKibbin neither; and especially down in the badlands. *They* won't be against us."

All his life with us Dad had ranted and railed against the badlanders. Let some rider from Enterprise or one of the big brands come around for a meal and he couldn't spread it on good enough, but let it be a poor fellow from down on the river and he'd be just barely civil. However, any old port in a storm! and he didn't object.

"You got your money?" I asked.

"Money! Where would I get money? I ain't been paid since June."

Nevertheless I knew he had more than a hundred dollars hid away, saving against his old age. I left him alone so he could get it. Even though we might never come back he wouldn't want to reveal the hiding place. I found an old saddle with the skirts gone, only the wood and hair for a seat, but with the rings, stirrups, etc. I made a cinch of clothesline which by passing back and forth could be drawn like a block and tackle; in fact I could have cut Old Hazel in half, but I wanted a good, solid seat for Dad. In the meantime he had gathered a couple of sacks of belongings which I put behind him. I got him well seated, with his boots in the stirrups, and I handed him his old needle gun, and he felt better, ready to face the unknown at age fifty-six; and I tied some more stuff on behind and in this tatterdemalion condition we set forth, under the blazing noon.

Stopped for a look at Ma's grave. They'd chose the turnip patch where they figured the new digging wouldn't show. Got off and doffed my hat because it was the decent thing to do. Her fate didn't seem so bad, really, even being tossed into the ground like a sack of meat, an animal, because nothing's so clean as our Western earth. Can be used on open sores for a poultice. Nothing lasts forever, that's what Rusty said. "Observe the clamshells of the hills," he told me. "Of the sea was it born and to the sea will it return." So much for that.

We could see their tracks. Fell in and follered. They didn't take the least precautions. Not a worry in the world. Didn't even take to the sod, but chose the gumbo patches. There were nine or ten of them. They didn't seem headed any place in particular. Kept to them in a general sort of a way across a completely empty land. Then of a sudden I knew I was being watched. That "seventh sense derived from our savage ancestors" made me pull to.

"What you see?" asked Dad.

They were the last words he ever spoke. *Thump!* a bullet hit him. The *whack!* a rifle makes in hot air of noon came an instant behind. He simply slid off his horse, uttering scarcely a sigh. The bullet passed right through him and kicked up dirt giving me a line on where the gun was. I could have told anyway. A wisp of smoke hung in the sunshine. Also, it is next to impossible for people to hide amid our mirage and heat-shimmer. You always see *something*, though I hadn't seen it in time. They had doubled back and laid for us.

Old Hazel went bucking away, and strange to say I took the risk of catching her. They shot at me, or rather in my general direction, sort of for the looks of things, to hasten me on my way, but it was plain they wanted me alive—alive and by my lonesome.

Leading Hazel I got out of range and watched while four men rode forth. They rode right over and looked at Dad, a solitary heap, and they passed his needle gun around, and they went through his belongings. I could tell when they found his money and divided it, the end of his dreams.

Cripes, I thought bitterly, how things had worked out! Here was Dad killed, and Ma, and Ringbone, maybe the Preacher, the old home burned, our ranch left for the taking, best range in the country to be pre-empted by Enterprise Land & Cattle, and all because of me. Because I had laid the trail that brought the Brigadier back, and even hung Grace's kerchief on a twig, thinking it so clever at the time.

> "Oh, what a tangled web we weave
> When first we practice to deceive!"

The sun beat down too hard for regrets. My present problems took precedence. I had been spared—why? Plainly because they had need of me. Which is to say McKibbin did. He still thought I could lead him to Grace and Rusty. I had fooled him, all right. Oh, I'd convinced him! And now my problem was *uncon-vincing* him! I wished she'd send him a card from Oregon, or somewhere, like a proper and forgiving daughter should, now they were safe away; otherwise he'd stick with me till hell froze. I took some modest satisfaction in how I'd fooled him, in spite of all. Chuckled about it as I rode. He had to believe they were still around to be caught, or he was beaten, and beaten was what he'd never admit himself to be.

"So I'm to lead you to 'em," says I. "Very well, let's make it a journey you'll never forget!"

I rode into the white glare of some alkali sinks. I kept a steady clip across the sinks, then out across a land of gnarled sagebrush high enough to slap my boots. A golden dust rose and plugged my nostrils.

Up jumped a deer. Gad, it scared me! It was a doe and she'd been taking her rest from the heat at the pocket end of a little draw. No ambushers here, she told me. The prairie was cut up by similar draws, they got larger, and I descended into the broken lands. I rode over sandrock in slabs and shards. Very hard on Old Hazel, who was unshod. Then my faithful Keno started to limp. I got down and saw he had a loose shoe and pebbles had got under it. Our saddle stock was cold shod, i.e. the shoes weren't burned on. We did it on the range, using shoes of cast metal which bent tight in use. However, they tend to loosen and have to be nailed again. Had no tool, not even a six shooter, the cowboy's hammer. Dug out the pebbles with my busted clasp knife. I was being watched. I couldn't see anything, and I can't say I *felt* it, as is supposed to happen. I knew it was a matter of logic. They weren't going to let me off that easy. I stopped. Couldn't make out a thing. Dismounted and had a look at the sky. This is a trick I'd learned long before, from Pa, or somebody. The sky is too bright to see much at that hour, so you look through your hat. The best felt always develops tiny pinpoint holes and if you look and look, using patience, the sky comes out slate blue, and there, in that tiny bit of it you will see birds. You always do. The sky no less than the earth is full of life. Eagles and hawks and smaller birds without number. The traveler stirs things up—snakes, gophers, etc., and the birds know it, and keep up with him aloft. Holding Old Hazel, I lay down on my back. Elbows propped, I could hold the hat absolutely still and the sun came through the pinholes like motes. And there were the birds, veering around and around, over me, and over something farther back, just as I had expected. Tried to guess the distance. I could have, too, if I'd known how high they were. You see, they were always at ninety degrees to the ground. There are instruments that will measure such things right to the foot. Artillerymen have them. I'll bet the Brigadier could have done it. You have to have an education to get to be field grade officer in the Army. It was one of the reasons Rusty hated McKibbin so—his learning. Envy, you might say. Rusty never even got as far in school as I did. The circuit teacher lived with us for three years, and I boarded in at Steele. Went through all McGuffey's Eclectics. Rusty wouldn't even listen to Ma read Scott, Fenimore Cooper, Lorna Doone, etc. Said it was just a pack of lies. He liked poetry, strange to say. He was practically on his own from age ten on. Cecil and Clint spoiled him. Then he blamed Ma for not sending him to school. "You could do things for you," Ma said to me. "Nobody could do anything for Russell."

Dallied a while, and, sure enough, my pursuer appeared. Not truly a pursuer. One man, not trying to catch up, but just to foller along. See where I was going. It was McKibbin. I knew by how he rode. Stiff and erect, not like your cowboy, who slouches and becomes part of his horse, riding with the least effort possible as befits a calling said to be the laziest on earth. I could tell it wasn't a stock saddle under him, it wasn't forward heavy to stand the weight of a steer hitting a rope, but just a place to sit, with stirrups and straps to hang things to. Waited for others to appear, but he was by himself. He wanted no witnesses to his daughter's disgrace.

"Quite an honor!" says I with a bitter laugh. "Henry Irons is to be one-against-one with the great McKibbin!"

He saw I'd stopped, so he stopped. He got off and had a look at me. Using a spyglass. Wanted to see if I was armed, and with what. It was a good glass, you could bet on that. With a thirty power glass, even at that distance, he could count the buttons on my shirt.

Remounted and rode on. Crossed over a ridge and had a look over the crest, hidden by bushes. Here he came, taking his time. Still by his long lonesome.

I could lose him at night if it was moonlight and I found a good, hard bottom. He could track me, but it would take a lot of time. Once at the river I could swim across to the Indian lands. Move in with the Blackfeet, learn their ways. Find myself a dusky bride, a chief's daughter like Rusty told about when he was adopted by the Flatheads.

Darkness found me I knew not where. You might say I was lost. Hunkered in for the night. When you sleep without blankets always try to find a real steep bank facing southwest. Clay holds heat. Don't try to lie down. Sleep sitting, with heels propped. Woke up before the sun. Very thirsty. Wondered where McKibbin was and how he had fared. Had his men showed up to make a camp for him? or had he spent the night like I? Very thirsty. Had lunch but no canteen. Managed to eat boiled egg and biscuit, the last of what Dad had put up. The yolk stuck in my throat like dry earth. I must have been half an hour getting enough spit to swaller it down. The horses smelled water and set out, but all they found was a flat place where a number of peet-weet birds ran around long-legged. These birds are a sure sign of water, but this time it lay a foot or more down and you'd have to dig to find seepage. Nothing to dig with, only fingers and the old, busted jackknife.

There was nothing to do but keep riding. Kept bearing with the morning sun on my right hand, generally north. Then, lo and behold! I saw one of Rusty's marks! It was a cigarette paper he had twisted around a top twig of sage, and it had lasted through wind and rain all since spring.

No doubt now where everything was located, and how I could find water. Wasn't about to share my secret, however. Vowed to wait until dusk. Found a cutbank with a narrow strip of afternoon shade. Got off and sat. Dozed despite thirst and pitiless heat. Then alarm jolted me like a snake buzz. I looked up and there sat the Brigadier on his big, bay horse looking down on me!

Chapter
Twenty-two

He that is without name, without friends, without coin, without country, is still at least a man; and he that has all these is no more.

—**Rob Roy**

"**B**oy!"
I lay, powerless to stir.
"Boy!" he says again.
"Huh?"
"Where's my daughter?"
"Who?"
"Don't you know who I am?"
I knew, all right, but my thoughts swam. "I guess so."
"I'm Major McKibbin."
Used his regular Army rank, not his brevet, which was Colonel, or Brigadier General, which they had honored him with in at Helena.
"Boy! Buck up! Pay attention!" It was terribly hard to focus on him in the fiery sun. "Where's my daughter?"
"I don't know!"
This was true; however, I knew I'd *better* know or be of no further use to him.

"You're lying, boy! You know and you're going to lead me!"

"She ain't down *here*. She ain't anywhere close. She left the country."

"Where's your brother?"

"Who?"

"Your brother! Get your wits about you."

"Which brother you talking about? I got —"

"Stop that!"

"I was just tryin' to tell you—"

"I'll not put up with that snotting and whining."

"All right," I whimpered.

"Stop it!"

I made a noise like a chicken, a long wheezing gasp, and pointed at my throat, hoping I'd get offered a drink. I figured he'd have to give me a drink if I couldn't talk.

"Boy, stop that!"

"E-e-e!" I went.

"You were all right a minute ago. Answer my questions and I'll give you some water."

He waited for my answer. Sat and rolled a cigar around in his mouth. Pity was unknown to him.

"Where's your brother, *Russell?*"

"I don't know where. He left the country."

"You were on your way to meet him."

"He left the country. That's the God's truth."

He didn't believe me. "Where's your destination?"

"My what?" I knew what a destination was, but preferred to act ignorant. "I don't own one, not as I know. All I got is what you can see, these two horses and my old—"

"Where were you headed?" he ripped out.

"Down to the river."

"Why? What's at the river?"

Water! I thought of saying, but decided not to make any smart rejoinders. "I was tryin' to get away. They tried to kill me. Somebody killed Ma and burnt our house. They killed Dad."

"Don't lie—your father died two years ago."

"Dad, not Pa. Dad Marsh. They shot him right off his horse. Laid in ambush and shot him in cold blood."

"And who do you suppose did all this?"

"The sheriff and his rangers, maybe. They served papers on Ma and she tore 'em up."

"Why did you go back there?"

"Go where?"

"To your home!"

"Because I live there!"

"I think you went home for supplies."

I stared at him as if, yep! he'd guessed it.

"What did you need the supplies for?"

"I was going to leave the country. I told you—"

"Who were you taking the supplies to?"

"I didn't get anything. Just a lunch Dad fixed."

"You went to get it for your brother, isn't that true?"

I didn't answer.

"Are they living down on the river?"

"I already told you I didn't—"

"Stop that! Stop whining!" Gad! he looked at me with contempt.

"You're lying to me, boy, and doing a poor job of it."

I stood there gaping.

"If you were headed for the river you'd have taken the old freight road down Cottonwood, and been there long since."

True, I would have. It would have been hail and farewell straight from the ranch.

"You deliberately headed into this Godforsaken land. They have a secret hiding place."

I pretended yes, he had me! I was no match for him. I cringed around like liars do when caught. In the books Ma read to us the liars always buckled.

He pulled out a slim, long-barrelled pistol all silvered shining in the sun. "Now I want the truth!" and he cocked it, *click! click!*

"All right! They have a place they go. It's a little, pocket valley nobody else knows about. It used to be a rustler's hangout when they drove horses through from Dakota. There's a log house. They used to meet there."

This was far from being music in his ears, so he barked out, "Where is this place?"

"To the west of here."

"How far west of here?"

"Three or four hours. I was just fixing to turn off."

"That's poison sink country. Cattle get in there and die."

"Just the same it's where they are! Where they *said* they'd be. They said—"

"Nobody could live there."

"Rusty could!"

"Oh, he could?"

"You bet!"

"Proud of your brother?"

"Yes."

"Even after the trouble he's caused your family?"

"He always treated me good."

I didn't want to antagonize him or challenge him, but I didn't want to seem entirely spineless, either. Don't get me wrong, I'd have licked his spit if I thought it would win for me, but for all that I had to be an *Irons.* I walked a crumbly edge.

221

"Loyalty!" He gave his lips a sour twist. "Loyalty, while admirable, can be sadly misplaced."

"How about that drink of water?"

"In what manner are they living?"

"Huh?"

"Are there others? Is there a settlement? A badlanders' place?"

"No. It's just a pocket valley and a cabin. It's a place called the Hole in the Wall."

"There's no such thing as the Hole in the Wall. That's a tall tale, Henry." He used my name instead of *boy*, showing a slight softening. Also, he lowered his gun, took it off cock.

"Rusty always called it the Hole in the Wall!"

"We shall see."

"What are you aiming to do with them?"

"Don't concern yourself with that. Your brother didn't concern himself with you, did he? Or with your mother."

"I dunno."

"Think about it. You say your mother was killed. Your faithful old cook was killed. Your house was burned. Is that so?"

"Uh-huh."

"Why was the sheriff after him? Not my doing. Wasn't it the result of sharp practices in his estray business? Always trying to get the edge? And who was left holding the sack? Then when the time came he abandoned you. Now get on your horse."

"How about my drink of water?"

He had two canteens. One was a regular Army canteen and the other a horse canteen, or water skin. He took the smaller one and sloshed the water around and had a swig, eyeing me to see how greedy I was. Then he put the top back on.

"No," he says, "you'll get a drink as soon as you have proved you're not lying."

"Please, please. I get dizzy in the heat. It's why I had to stop here and lie down. I couldn't make it in the sun. I can't even stay on my horse."

"Stop that!"

"Then give me a drink like you promised."

Zing! he cut me with his quirt. Not *cut* as brings blood, like a knife, but a sharp stroke across neck and shoulder. I'd been around quirts all my life and never been hit by one. It was so vicious and unexpected I didn't have time to get a hand up. It truly shocked me: it was uncalled for, and unfair. I suppose you could say I was disappointed in him.

"Don't whine! When I tell you something, obey!"

He was about to come at me again. Getting back, I fell to my haunches. This put me out of whip range. I crawled around a sagebrush. However, he was finished with just the one lick.

"Stop cringing! What your kind needs is a course of military discipline! This country allows too much freedom. People are not called to account. They get to thinking the land owes them a living. It owes them nothing. They call themselves free and equal. Freedom has to be won, and equality earned. Do you understand what I'm saying?"

"Guess so."

"Then stand up and stop whining."

I did, and caught Old Hazel.

"What's wrong with her hoofs?" he asked.

"Bruised. She ain't been shod."

"Is that how you treat horses?"

"She was the only one left at home. They ran all of 'em off."

"She looks like a fair horse. Unsaddle her."

"Huh?"

"When I give an order, obey it! Unsaddle her!"

I did so.

"Turn her loose."

I did, and she drifted away. She'd head for home, I supposed.

"If there's one thing I can't countenance it's a person who owns horses and neglects them."

Yet he expected me to ride Old Keno, loose shoe and all!

"Now, what's wrong with *him?*"

"One loose shoe."

"Well, remove it!"

"How can I? I ain't got a tool."

He handed me a pocket knife with a heavy blade and a hook for pulling nails. Must have weighed a pound. I might have sprung on him but he had his eye on me. I'd have had to open the blade first. Wouldn't have stood a chance. I tied Keno close up against a sage, the only thing handy, and managed to get his foot in my lap, and after some lunging around get the rest of the nails out. The shoe had worn so thin it bent double in the process. McKibbin looked with contempt at that, too.

I gave him back his knife and we set out. Keno limped, but more from habit than loss of the shoe. The sun had swung around and we rode into it. I kept my hat down and watched the ground.

"Where's the trail?" asked McKibbin.

"Ain't none. Supposed to take a different way each time."

This piece of logic seemed to yield me credit. Leastwise he didn't rag me for a time. The late sun reflected off the ground right back in my face and I had to stop, my wounded head still aflame.

"What's the trouble?"

"I was shot through the head by a stray bullet. I can't keep on my horse."

Zing! came the quirt. "You weren't shot through the head. No man is and lives. Keep going!"

"I can't, not without water."

He had the choice of whipping me or giving me a drink, so he chose the latter. Only he didn't offer me the canteen. He poured some on a handkerchief and handed me that.

"Put it in your mouth."

I did, and sucked on it until I got out the water and it dried. "You want this back?"

"No, that's my gift to you." He'd no more have touched that handkerchief now than he'd have handled a snake.

"Please, give me some more."

With what stony contempt he looked at me! He took a swig from the canteen, watching me all the while, and swished it around in his mouth, and then he spit it out. See how I take the heat? he seemed to be saying. See what true fortitude is?

We went on again. The country was all pretty much the same. I kept thinking I recognized a scene or landmark but I couldn't be sure. And there, slam in my face, was one of my signs! It was the top two twigs of a sage I'd looped together. McKibbin never noticed a thing. For once I was smarter than he was. Gave me a new strength. Needed it. Rode on and on straight into the sun. Deep into the afternoon and I wondered if I was lost. Now and then I'd see some landmark or place that seemed familiar, but shrunken, flatter, and all bleached. The squaw currants that had been such a webby, live green with pinkish blossom were now only brown with here and there an orange berry.

Grabbed a berry here and there and ate. Sour and seedy.

I saw the eagles' nests with their white streaks of droppings, like whitewash dumped from above by some mighty hand.

"Where are you going?" his voice cracked out the first time in many a mile.

"Toward them rocks."

"Don't make a fool of me, boy!"

"I ain't! This here is the way!"

To make a long story short, I led him up and around the big fallen rocks, found the deer droppings, and felt at last the draught of wind and smell of a different region, and the cliff parted.

I didn't need to tell him this was it, this was the famed Hole in the Wall. He was awed in spite of himself.

Chapter Twenty-three

"I think," said Lord Gudyill, "they hae found the falcon's neb a bit overhard for them. It's no for naught the hawk whistles."

—*Old Mortality*

He was suspicious. Expected a trick. Thought Rusty would have sentries out, had a gang backing him, badlanders, his own Hole-in-the-Wall gang. Thought I might be leading him into a trap. Drew his pistol. Previously described, it was one of a brace, fine, ivory-handled pieces. Cocked it, pointed it in my direction, warning that in case of duplicity I'd be first to die.

"Proceed!"

Did so, having to urge the horses. Never anxious to enter closed places. As previously stated, your horse off the range will balk at being led into shed or barn even. Cool twilight inside the hole, or cleft. You could see the sun where it reflected, but not the sky. Bats or something moved and you could see the flutter, or the shadow of it. Then we came out into the sun again, scene marvelously changed. There was the valley and cliffs.

And I could smell smoke! It was a camp smell. *Whoa!* halted then and there. Naturally McKibbin did, too.

I don't know whether he could smell it or not. Cigar smoking is very dulling to the olfactory. I knew I could smell things Rusty never suspected, he being heavily addicted to cigarettes. In the dead of night I could recognize people by their smell. This was an advantage I had. And, believe me, I needed every small advantage I could muster! A multitude of thoughts raced through my mind as to what this smoke could be. It might possibly be just the baked smell from the late summer sun, doubtful; or it could be one of those places in the bad lands where the coal seams catch on fire and burn under the earth, emitting smoke to the vagrant breeze; or it could be rustlers, or Indians, the Blackfeet were ever sneaking over from the reserve to butcher a beef and then sneak back again; and then, it could be Rusty! Yes, it could be Rusty and his bride. They could have doubled around to Rocky Point, or Cottonwood Landing, Coalbank or some other post supplied by steamboat, and come back for a stay, what was called the "honey-moon." The thought of it made me almost buckle. Actually went sweaty despite lack of moisture.

"Boy! What's the matter with you?"

"I think we ought to get out of here!"

He never moved. Thought it was a trick.

"I'm afeard there's somebody down there. It could be the Dakota gang!"

"What Dakota gang?"

"The horse thieves! They run 'em from Minnesota all the way to the gold camps!"

"No, they haven't been active in years. All that is a thing of the past."

He got out his spyglass and swept slowly the bottoms. All around were the most savage of cliffs, but they closed on meadows, trees, etc.

"Ah-ha!" I thought for a second he was going to hand me the glass. "Cookfire!" And with just a note of acknowledgement, "You do have your wits about you after all!"

He'd seen it, not smelled it. And soon, without the glass, I could see it, too. A bluish haze under the trees, purplish as the evening came.

"Well, boy!" He was much pleased with me, and with himself. "Now you may have your drink."

He swished the Army canteen, had a swig himself, poured some on the ground, handed the remainder to me, and I took it down in about four swallers.

We still had quite a wait. He seemed in no doubt I'd led him to them, and didn't want to take any chances. I wasn't so sure. I was afraid it wouldn't be them, and afraid it would. Either might be bad for me. Which would be worse, well, that was a question!

One thing was sure, I had to do as he said. McKibbin might have relented as far as the drink of water was concerned, but I was still untrusted, still at gunpoint, after a manner of speaking. Well could I imagine my fate once he decided I was tricking him, and of no further use. *Bang!* that would be the end of me!

He looked at his gold flip-open pocket watch. Finest watch in the land. Had to check and see whether the sun was going down on time. Ridiculous, but in a sense true. The sun sets earlier in the hills and mountains. Out on the prairie one stands on a bulge. This is a fact, the world being round, not round like a saucer

229

as it seems on the prairie, but round like a ball, and you're always on its highest part.

So much for that. *Click!* went the watch. "Remount!"

I did so.

"Proceed!"

Not on the trail. He gestured otherwise. It was no fit trail anyhow. After the first flat area, where old manure could be seen, but a number of trails. This had been deliberate on the part of previous horsemen. "A snare awaits the otter that follers the same trail twice." This is a quote, from Fenimore Cooper. Ma read us from Cooper as well as Sir Walter, and there was much in his books of use to the Western outdoorsman. We went sliding downhill, as Rusty and I had on the previous occasion, until sitting a horse became too dangerous. Your steep country is ill suited to the so-called centerfire saddle, which I had. The General's cavalry rig was much better, with its forward cinch, or rimfire style. A true mountain saddle is double cinched, full rimfire Colorado style, and even sometimes with crupper and martingale, but few were seen in our parts and the horses hate them. Whatever your rig it is always safest to dismount and walk, as previously noted, keeping to one side, so if your horse slips he doesn't come down and brain you with his forefeet, and this we did, yours truly taking the lead so I couldn't slip away to freedom.

Finally our way gentled off and we found ourselves in a little, grassy field where horses had grazed. You could see where picket stakes had been driven and they had eaten in perfect circles each in diameter exactly double the length of the rope. This was one hundred feet. In Montana most cowboys use the full fifty foot lariat, and take dallies, or wraps, around the saddle horn when they catch a calf. The Southern boys are more likely to use a shorter rope tied fast. Hence your range detective may be able to look at a picket circle and tell where a cowboy came from.

"H-m!" says McKibbin.

Dark was coming fast, now. Much shorter twilights once it gets towards fall. This had been the driest and hottest in memory.

"You say this is a basin?"

"Yes."

"No stream outlet?"

"None."

He believed me when we kept to one of the gullies and came down on the tarn, or sink. I already told about the alkali, and yellow stuff, and the foul stench. It was that bad our horses pulled back, thirsty though they may have been.

"That material could be valuable," he said, meaning the alkali. "It contains the element sodium. They pay good money for that over at the silver mines."

You see how his mind worked. Here he was pursuing his daughter, and for aught he knew walking into a trap, but part of his mind schemed for money.

"This country provides many opportunities for the poor man aside from branding another's cattle." Then he added, "Your mother was a fine woman." So much for the Ironses.

The smoke came stronger, with the fresh smell of evergreen, or pitch wood. They seemed to be burning juniper. Quaking asp makes an almost smokeless fire, and men on the skulk favor it, showing how little they worried about being caught. And soon the smell of bacon frying.

"Suppertime," says I, and he looked at me with, oh!

what cold hatred. I had reminded him of their conjugal relations, being together, laughing and talking together, eating together, sleeping together.

"Take care of the horses!"

Did so. He would tell me to do this and do that and I'd hop and do it. Couldn't figure what he had in mind, in the dark. If they left the fire burning it would guide him, but if they put it out, as they most assuredly would, why, it would be dark as the pit. The moon would rise but it gave a poor light; at home, on the familiar ground, you could see to walk by moonlight, but here, amid the brush and gullies, and all the trees and fallen rock, all strange, it would be impossible.

Gave each some water from the horse canteen, which was of leather, and opened out. Gave a sparing quart or so to his horse, whose name was Ranger, and a smaller amount to my own Keno. He was kind to animals, I'll say that for him. He himself rubbed down Ranger with a piece of gunny sacking carried for the purpose. He chose a place for them to be picketed, a small piece of grass and bramble surrounded by bullberry bushes. All the while he watched me very close, because it was the time when the eyes plays tricks, and shadows move, and I might make a break for it.

Their voices came, a girl's bright laughter and a word from Rusty—I knew his voice—close as at the elbow, such were the tricks the evening played with sound. Then silence. They'd probably turned in. No candle light.

"Here, boy!" He spoke to me like he might Duke, his curly retriever. "Empty your pockets."

Did so, dumping what I had on the ground—three .41 calibre pistol cartridges, my old jackknife with the

232

blade busted, a brass button for luck, and three silver dollars. He looked at this sorry wealth. Only the .41's seemed to interest. Each cartridge had one of those bottleneck tacks which made it look like a .44, but wasn't.

"Take the money back."

Did so, and he swept all the rest off into the gloom with a sweep of boot.

"Walk over here."

Did so.

"Lie down."

Obeyed, on my back with hands under head, looking at him.

"On your face!"

Rolled over.

"Hands behind you."

Did so.

"Cross your wrists."

I was doing this, in an awkward position, face in the dirt, when he pounced on me like a puma. Not right *on* me, but with a foot on each side. He fastened my wrists together before I knew what had happened. You see, if a person knew what he was about he might be able to turn over and deliver him a two-legged kick to the crotch. But of course I missed my chance, being unprepared. He knew all the risks through his years of leading troops against the Indians.

I twisted and fought to no avail. Couldn't see how he'd fastened me so quick. What he'd used was a strap with buckle. A narrow strap, but I couldn't hope to bust it.

"Test it, boy!"

So I stopped. He fastened me across the elbows, by rope. He tied me by one elbow to a bush. When I tried to jerk free the top waved against the sky.

"The harder you fight that slip noose the tighter it's going to be."

No matter what I did it was what he expected me to do, and I stopped because the rope across my elbows was fairly pulling my shoulders out of joint.

"You better lie still, boy!"

"Can't breathe!" I gasped.

"You can *talk!*" he says, disgusted.

"Let me go, dang you!"

Whang! he hit me alongside the head. Hit me with a gun!

"No more of that!"

Spent some time trying to breathe, get rid of dizziness.

"Boy!"

Guess he thought I'd passed out. Didn't want me dead. Wanted me as a lure to Rusty. A judas sheep.

"Loosen up. I can't breathe."

He deigned to poke his toe under my head. Sprung it around some. Could taste the boot leather. Wondered if he intended to gag me. I'd heard of this though never seen it done. Never saw a man tied up before, either—except for Rusty, when he was cowwhipped.

"Don't try to call out."

I kept wheezing in a sort of a whistle, I must have sounded like a young cockerel starting to crow. It couldn't have been very loud. Seemed to amuse him somewhat.

"I don't want to knock you on the head, boy. Boy, listen to me. I don't want to have to split your skull."

What did he expect from me, the Soldier's Oath of Allegiance?

I gasped out an "Aw-right," or something like; at least he seemed satisfied.

* * *

So there I lay, and he went off someplace. It was very dark by now, not even the hint of a moon. I must have slept, or passed out. Woke up with my arms dead to all feeling. Tried to open and close my hands. Recalled the tale of a cowboy over on the Goose Bill that was caught under his fallen horse and developed mortification in one leg, died of it. They could smell that leg for half a mile. A horrible thing to think about. Kept trying and trying to open my hands, close them, get the circulation going. That's how my night passed, not in pain, and not in thirst, just numbness.

Kept coming to. Came to maybe a hundred times, with terrible imaginings in between. That's how the night passed. Sometimes the moon was out, and again it wasn't. And it paled toward dawn. I had such dreams I wasn't sure whether there'd been a day and it was night again, or what. It was like being sick for a week with fever. I was being talked to. I came up through several layers of misery and says, "What?" through cracked and fevered lips.

"Boy?"

"Uh-huh."

"Turn over."

I couldn't do it. I couldn't more than flail around with my legs. He did it for me, with a rough lift with one hand and a boot toe. Fussed around with my bonds. He had untied and unbuckled me, but I couldn't get my arms to work.

"They're mortified."

"What's that?"

"I say they're dead. They're mortified."

"Don't be a damned fool."

He got me up on my pins and caused me to walk,

and he took me shambling by a lasso or something about my neck, straight over toward the spring, and where Rusty's camp was, and stopped under a big old bullberry, not in any grove, an old one out by itself. He tossed the free end over a limb, pulled me right up by the neck, like he was going to hang me, and tied off the loose end. Lucky the noose wasn't a slip knot this time, but even so I could just barely breathe. What I said came as a sort of a whistle.

"Can you breathe?"

"No!"

And he laughed in his disgusted way, stuck two fingers in, testing, not because he had to, but because he was kindly, blessed with sense of humor, etc.

"Can't breathe but you can talk, ha-ha."

What should I have done? turn blue in the face?

Here's a peculiar thing, though—I got to almost feeling gratitude toward him, he'd let me live so long!

All this while it had been growing lighter. It was a long way till dawn, but a reflection of sky and cliffs had commenced to erase the shadows. Realized I was out in the open with a view of the camp. *I* could see the old cabin. Then somebody came outside and saw *me*.

"Rusty!"

Leastwise I managed some sort of a sound and he saw me. He stood absolutely rooted to the spot in startlement.

"Rusty! Look out! Ambush!"

It's what I tried to say, and the warning in some manner must have gone out, because gad! did he get out of the way, and McKibbin had missed his chance.

McKibbin then spoke, not loud, but with an entreaty that carried, and I can still hear his voice:

"Grace? This is Papa."

She said something, probably to Rusty, and stole forth. Then she saw me and screamed.

Her father tried to quiet her saying it was all right, nothing would happen, that "his brother can free him and leave the country," and more of the kind, but she screamed and screamed. She had started and couldn't stop. You can imagine what a shock it was, to see somebody you knew hung there. His whole idea had backfired. Womankind is one thing the Army never learned how to handle.

Finally she got down where I couldn't see her, although her sobbing could be heard, and she quieted down, and I was still there with the problem of staying alive. My noose was tightening, not getting looser. Actually it was the pressure from above. What was happening, I since decided, was the branch which had loosed, and become more supple in the night, with the cool and damp, had started to shrink and lift in the first warmth of the sun.

Figured I was a goner. My sight started to go, all black and flickering, and *whack!* A thing hit right above, I can't recall hearing a rifle, but the branch flew splinters. I could feel the shake from head to toes, and *whack!* once more.

You read and hear about people riding up to rescue the hanged just as they are swung off, and shooting the rope in half. Folly, of course. Buffalo Bill type of yarn. No ordinary calibre can shoot a rope in half. Lucky to cut one strand. You might with a shotgun loaded with number two at about ten feet. Anyway, what Rusty was doing was relieving the branch. Every time a bullet hit it I got more breath. It lowered me so I could get my feet back on Mother Earth. With this purchase I somehow managed to get my head free of the noose, almost tearing my ears off (I actually

237

found scabs of blood under both lobes) and made the ground where I crawled away, escaping through the bushes like a legless animal. Covered at least sixty yards until Rusty says, "Hey, there!" right above me.

"What you think you are, a woodchuck?"

Always a joke. Covered with dirt and litter I must have been quite a sight.

"Well, little brother," he says, "what are you doing in these out-of-the-way parts?" And he says, "Who's your friend?"

He meant the Brigadier. Can't say I was in any mood for repartee.

"Very nice of you to bring him here," he said with sarcasm.

"How'd I know you were here? You was supposed to be in Idaho."

He considered this excuse. I can imagine how it must have struck him, coming forth and finding me there with the Brigadier, just as if I'd been guiding him to Rusty's lair.

"I was trying to lose him! I figured I'd get away in the night. Figured he'd be days finding his way back."

"How are things at home?"

He must have got wind of what had happened. I guessed he'd been at one of those outlaw towns around Coalbanks and come here until things quieted. I told him in brief about Ma, and being burnt out, and about how they'd shot poor Dad Walsh and taken his needle gun, savings, etc., but I could see his mind was elsewhere. Never cared a fig for Dad. They hadn't got along. Rusty would have him cook this or that and he'd put too much salt in it. He pulled out tobacco and papers.

"Roll one?"

"Fingers too swole."

"Do it for you."

"I might have a chaw."

I had chewed tobacco before. I'd hated the taste and it made me sort of sick, but it had encouraged the flow of spit, which I figured I might swaller. I was truly parched, not having had a drink of water since the evening before, and then not much.

"So here we are, the last of the Ironses," says Rusty.

"Last on the old range, at any rate."

"Last cigarette," he says with a grin.

"Last chaw."

It sure seemed good to be so close to him, brothers at the final go-round, but I got to wondering why this was the last? Didn't we have the Brigadier two to one?

"I want you to take care of Grace for me."

I must have looked blank.

"I want you to get her out of here!" he said roughly. "Take her to the Landing. It's time for the autumn rise, take a boat. Go to Benton. Go to Helena, or Spokane Falls. Go to Oregon. I'll trace you. I have my ways."

"Just leave you here?"

"Yes, just leave me here. What's the matter, kid, don't you think I can take care of myself?"

Oh, I thought that, all right! He wanted to be left one-on-one with the Brigadier. He plans to kill him, I thought, and he doesn't want her around to view the act. It simply made my blood flow cold. You'd think I'd be proof against any such aversion after all I'd gone through, but this was different. Why, it's his own child's grandfather, his child-to-be. However, I didn't let on.

"Take this."

It was some money, mostly paper, some gold.

"Grace has some too. She'll be waiting past the house."

He smoked his cigarette and I mine. Wasn't exactly what I needed after long thirst. My mouth felt and tasted like it did one time after fighting a range fire.

"Wish I had a rifle," I said, speaking more or less to myself.

"What happened to the one I gave you?"

"Lost it."

He didn't try to hide his disgust. "Pistol, too?"

"Yes, I was shot. They hit me in the head."

Didn't give credence. I showed him my hat, with the big hole bashed through, and the place on my skull still not healed, all swole with prickly hairs to be picked out with matter in the roots.

"My ears still ring when I move sudden."

"No, I'm not giving you another gun. You'll be better off without one. Guns are the curse of this country."

An amazing statement, but there it was. With it he spit out his cigarette and rose to one knee. He'd been looking at something, and peering, for some time. What he could see were Ranger and Old Keno away off in the brush. They were mostly hid, but their heads and eyeballs were plain when they raised to look around as horses do when they rise from eating, and shake flies, and snort, and view a strange country.

Rusty wet his thumb and brushed the front sight of his rifle, which was a bead sight, and had a way of gathering dust. He lifted it and *whang!* he shot with the barrel so close to the side of my head I felt like it had been carried off all over again.

It came as an absolute surprise, and I had a glimpse of Ranger being hit. He went down like he'd been hit by a sledge. He must have turned clean over on his back because I could see all four hoofs fly in the air.

"Hey!" I yelled and reached for the rifle, because I see he was going to shoot Old Keno as well. Too late, he shot again, did it while batting me aside with the rifle barrel, and the powder flew past.

Never will it leave my mind's eye how Keno went down, slow as almost with a sigh, just sort of settling to earth, his life's travels o'er.

"Why'd you do that?"

He didn't deign to answer. However, I can be stubborn and wouldn't move until he answered.

"Listen, kid, there's nothing that brings a cavalryman down to earth like being set afoot."

"Where's your horse?"

"You miss the whole point."

I saw what he meant: both he and McKibbin were to be afoot; head and head, equal at last. Had to concede it was a devilish idea.

"Now, get a-goin! Skedaddle."

So I did. Skulked along seeking cover, came out with a view of the cabin, passed by, had a drink from the spring, where it ran off filling the hoof tracks and sunk away. Saw the neat print of a woman's boot. Reached the place indicated by Rusty—a slice of bald rock under which a trail ran; no horses there but fresh sign, follered it, and finally there she was, sitting high up on old Maccabee, with a ginger roan gelding and a muley packhorse on lead string. Extra saddle, not the surcingle Rusty had set out with. This was a different horse, too, it wore a Rocking Chair brand. She had some of the baggage she'd had handed down off the coach, ill roped down.

"Come on!" she said without ado. "Let's get going!"

She was scared. No foolishment about her, she wanted to be out and away! If those two men, the dearest in her life, wanted to settle things, that was all right with her! Not cowardly, you understand. Just common sense. Fact of life. A woman in her condition must needs think not only of herself but of her child unborn.

Chapter Twenty-four

Man is not a tree, bound to one spot of earth:
Nor is he forced to cling to one bare rock, like
the scarce animated shell-fish. Thine own
Christian writings command thee, when
persecuted from one city, flee to another.
                                    —The Talisman

Break-leg country, Rusty called it. All blocky stone. On foot it wouldn't have been so bad, but on horseback—one false pull of the rein, and *crack!* It would mean another dead horse, and this one by my hand. I was armed: Rusty had left his six shooter with Grace, and she handed it over to me. Then we saddled and rode, supplies on a packhorse, as per instructions.

But so slow, slow with care. I sure wanted to leave the valley behind before the Brigadier saw what was happening and made his move to stop us. His being left afoot wouldn't stop him—not slow as we went!

"We better walk," says I, so we did, and I let Grace go ahead whilst watching the country behind.

We were at the so-called Iron Wall. This proved to be a gray sandrock turned blackish on the very surface by some sort of a coating, like what the prospectors call a manganese stain. Hours passed, it came midday and very hot as we wandered in and out at a pockety end of the valley. It was much bigger than I'd expected, but no other way offered safety; I didn't dare cross the bottoms. The sun beat on us. There had been no water at the old spring, only a barrel sunk in and withered. Rusty had packed water in a keg. We took one small whisky bottle full, and let the horses drink, hence there was hardly a swaller left. The Brigadier might have a few drops—by his fallen horse.

"Why did he do it, Hank?" she asked me. She simply pleaded that I tell her of Rusty's strange deeds. She took my hand and looked into my eyes. It wrenched the heart when she looked to me like that, and I felt stumbling and helpless to answer. "I guess there's something about when two horsemen meet afoot. It was the only way they could settle as equals."

"I don't want them to kill each other. I don't want either of them to die. Oh, Hank, I'd never love either if he killed the other!"

"Wasn't that just what Rusty said? Yes, he did." It seemed to me he had so spoken, or so indicated. "He wouldn't accept the report that your Pa burned up Ma." I see she hadn't heard about this. "And of course he hadn't! The house got on fire and he couldn't get her out. It was the sheriff to blame for attacking the place. Your Pa is a man of honor and so is Rusty. Rusty figured it was one way to come to an understanding as equals, man to man."

I could see she was simply sick about it, and she stayed with me even closer. She kept as close as it was possible for a girl to be, considering the rough and rocky ground.

"Rusty said straight out he expected your Pa would make his peace after his grandchild was born."

At last we got around all the dead-end dips. Came to the white sand-rock pillars and couldn't have been more than half a mile from the pass. We had a fine view, and I pulled in to rest the horses—which incidentally were not the same ones they'd left the Snowies with, but bore the Panhandle brand, and had been traded for, along with some other stuff, down at the Coalbanks.

I knew something had attracted my gaze—it was a movement on the bottom and there was the Brigadier. I knew him by his shape, or posture, and by the glint of his spyglass. I wondered if he was peering at us, far, far away. But no, the sun was wrong to make a glint, he was peering back across where we'd been, but higher up. And there was a man on a cliff-jut of the Iron Wall.

"Hey, General!" It was Rusty's wild call. "Hey, General!" and *general-general-general* from the echoes. "Here I am!"—*am-am-am!*

They stood and looked at each other for the longest time. Then Rusty did a wild dance and waved his rifle around.

"Come with me, General!" *(eneral-eneral-eneral)* "I'll show you the way out!" *(out-out-out)*.

I says to Grace, who watched this wild antic dumbfounded, "You see, they'll need each other. That's what makes the difference."

I found the pass after a bad scare. Took my time. Retreated and had a second try at it, remembering the trio of landmarks Rusty had once pointed out, had driven into my mind, it seemed with this very moment in view. I zigged and zagged until I got them— red stain of iron, drift of deadwood and the jagged pinnacle like an old legbone of massive scale—all

245

equal in angle, by what the land surveyors call the "triangulation of the thumb."

Still tarried a while. Had a last look below. Brushed out all our sign—tracks, horse manure, etc., using a wand. Didn't want to *hide* the exit, you understand, but didn't want to hang up a sign, "This way to the fleeing daughter and consort," either.

At last we entered the pass, the "hole in the wall." Had at that moment a most terrible premonition. Something would happen! Men would rise up and bar the way. Halt! or a sudden blast of guns, but it didn't happen. All was quiet. We emerged into sunshine and the silent eagles passed above—no other movement in all the vast, broken land. No fresh tracks: the Brigadier must have left hard instructions he was not to be follered. It was to be between him and Rusty, and he got what he'd came for.

It was a very hard thing to ride easy, take one's time, and not give the horses full rein, because they liked the downhill and would gladly have got out of there. I turned off the trail and took new ground to the river. This may seem risky, but a river is hard to miss. We slept side by side in a little hole the high water had scooped out. Found some fish in the shallows and caught a large sucker by hand, but had no matches for a fire. Famished and I'd have eaten some raw, but it seemed to make Grace sick, just the thought of it, and didn't wish to fall in her esteem.

We rode on and came to a woodcutter's cabin. He fed us and I gave him a dollar. Refused the dollar, but took it when I let him mend my boot sole which had come loose. We crossed some shallows no more than belly deep and took the north shore, preferring Blackfeet to some chance with men from the Long M who might be roaming under instructions.

"They'll take *my* orders!" says Grace with a flash of the eye, but I didn't want to chance it.

We got to Rocky Point and camped outside. I moved Grace to a camp where somebody had put up a lean-to and left again. Needed money because Rusty had forgotten and kept all they had in his clothes. Got a job dressing timbers for Mackinaw boats with adze at $2 per day, and could have ridden to Omaha, but didn't figure a Mackinaw boat was any place for a girl, although one man took wife and child (squaw and papoose, halfbreed.)

After some weeks, with money in pocket we went down the Benton road, slept in the open, and were passed by the stage. Turned off to the Belt Mountains and their famed gold camps, steered clear of Diamond City, came down on the Helena Valley, steered clear of Helena, also, and reached Cardiff atop the Continental Divide in a very depleted condition.

Decided to sell out. Saddle horses not in demand, here it was all work stock, broken to double harness, but we were paid in gold, which will always command better value than currency, and we sold the gear, saddles, bridles, packsaddle, etc., to an Englishman who was looking for that very thing.

I let Grace care for all moneys. This precaution I recommend to all young couples setting forth on life, which, after all, we were.

We were now far off from the old range, and could breathe easier. We went to Ophir and its sister camp of Blackfoot City, deep in the mining country, the land of gold. Little care here for drought, overgrazed range, and the alleged crimes of the Irons family. Prairie Montana could have seceded from the Union for all the gold miners cared. I rented a cabin and went to work in one of the placer mines two miles from Blackfoot City. Water was brought in many miles by flume. They had sluices raised twenty to thirty feet off the ground carrying torrents. Rocks as big as your head would hit a riffle, which were steel rails bought as scrap from the railroad, and *bong!* that rock might break right in half. When rocks lodged in the sluice you had to go along the catwalk and get them out. Although receiving the high wage of $4 per day of ten hours I said "No, thank you," because it was only a matter of time before you fell in. One man disappeared without a trace and was thought to have left the country, but later his boot nails were found at cleanup when they shut off the water to collect the gold. All else had been pounded to bits. These and other interesting objects of the placer mining lore were on display at one of the saloons.

Grace meanwhile got restive and took employment as waitress at the Gem Cafe. This was a decent place though often in uproar, Mrs. Appleton, the proprietress, being one of the camp characters. They would figure out things to say to her to get her in a fritz, and would she come back at them! Grace came in for it, too, but handled it well, and made as much "slinging hash" as I had tending sluice, and free meals to boot. This didn't include yours truly, but if I came in during the quiet times they'd serve me a steak for the same price as stew.

"You sure got things going your way," fellows would say to me. "You got the best looking wife in camp and nothing to do but keep tabs on her." "She can come over to my shack any time and no hash to sling, either," etc. Finally, however, she got to showing her condition, so we left and rode by sled through the first snow down to Garrison Junction on the N.P., there to board the Pacific Express for the Coeur d'Alene silver fields of Idaho, my first time ever on the cars, though Grace was an old hand. It was indeed a strange sensation to be whirled away at forty miles per hour over the singing rails, but I quickly steadied to it. Detrained at Baker Gulch and stayed at a hotel. Money easy to come by, many jobs, but prices were so high we couldn't save a cent. Bought a second-hand pistol, Colt patent side-hammer, .41 calibre. Had no fear of trouble from Montana, but the country was full of Pinkertons, Knights of Labor, and foreign anarchists, all violent types. Worked for a time at the White Elephant Stables. This place was run by an extremely fat man named Tom McClure who sat and read newspapers all day, and in these I saw various versions of the "Irons Range War." The follering is a sample which had been printed some time before, down in Green River, Wyoming, McClure's former home:

A LUCREZIA BORGIA
WESTERN STYLE

Thelma Irons of the Buffalo
Sinks Range has shot down a
Sheriff and Four Deputies!

And so on, with scarcely any truth. The Denver Rocky Mountain News had her as a buffalo hunter standing up against the advance of the cattle herds. However if you thought that was wild you should look at the Eastern papers. The Chicago Weekly Ledger had her leading the Hole in the Wall gang. Rusty and I were mentioned and were said to have been hung by vigilantes. (Eventually, a year or so later, when I was in Seattle, there was a book by Old Scout in the Buntline 5 cent Library called *Thelma Irons, Buffalo Queen of the Plains,* purporting to be the true story of her career. They had a picture on the cover that made her look like a girl pony express rider. Scarcely a true fact crept in. They had a character named "Sky Pilot" who spouted scripture while driving off whole herds of steers, robbing coaches, raiding steamboats, etc., who might have been Preacher Harlow. Ma was supposed to have had a tryst with Buffalo Bill and a rifle shooting contest with Calamity Jane, the winner to get Midnight, the greatest long horse in the West. It was preposterous.)

No mention of McKibbin in any of the newspapers. From time to time I ran into some Montana man from east of the Divide and I'd drop a question such as, "Whatever happened to that fellow, what was his name? McKibbin. Brigadier General. Did he ever get elected to Congress?"

"Oh, him!" they'd say after some thought. "No, I don't think he ran." Or they'd more likely confuse him with Roundhouse Jack McKibbin, the prizefighter, who went forty-two rounds with Burke, The California Slasher, in Butte City. *Sic transit gloria mundi!*

Much later I chanced to see a notice in the Lewiston, I.T. paper advertising some lots at auction to settle the estate of "Otis H. McKibbin, legally deceased." Legally meant they never turned up with his body. But nothing about Rusty. And as for us, we were

"—gone, aye, ages long ago,
Those lovers fled away into the storm."

After some hesitation I took the item and showed Grace, and she was saddened by it. "Still, you can't tell," she said. "He might turn up. It seems like they were in an awful hurry."

She didn't want to admit the truth. What Rusty had done was taunt him and leave him there. He had told me many times how a person could get down in the badlands and just walk around in circles, and die at last.

I still love the old range, and long for it, but this is my home now, and I like it, too. What I'm speaking of is the mighty arm of the sea known as Puget Sound. We lived at the small port of Arcadia, where our child was born, a son. Rusty's child, and he looked just like him, curly red hair and all. Grace said we should get married, now we're old enough, and we did, and she is to have a second child, our own. Naturally I regard the first-born as mine as well, because after all both will have the same set of grandparents—and a disparate lot they are! Or were. We moved to Seattle, up the Sound, a city on the march, counting no fewer than 4,000 souls, burgeoning as the capital of the canned salmon trade. My window on this busy world was enhanced when I found employment at Jerrud's Store, near which stands the famed Totem Pole. It is said that if one stands by Seattle's Totem Pole long enough, one will see every person in the Northwest as well as Alaska, "north of the Fifty-three." Hence keep thinking this to include Rusty and Uncle Will. Especially Uncle Will. Rusty I'm in two minds of, but I'd like to settle our affairs face to face. "We're wed," I figured I'd say to him, "and I'm not about to stand aside." But I anticipate no trouble. He's not the settling kind. Freedom becomes a way of life. He never would "put down roots and grow with the country."

I saw him once, or thought I did. "Rusty! Rusty!" I

yelled, but he had gone into a saloon, and when I busted in he wasn't there.

"Did you see a tall fellow come through here, look like a cattleman?"

"I saw a tall fellow, but I don't know about the cattleman part. He *hoosle* out the back door."

I never knew for sure. It was all timber, fishing and the sea. Half the time the butchers sold moose and caribou, passing it off as beef and buffalo. Yes, actually, you could order a buffalo steak and it would come up moose meat, with the musky swamp taste plain as day.

Grace is impatient to go home and see to it she gets her share of the estate, but from what I gather reading the Helena paper the Long M was much encumbered by debt. Like the Ironses, her father was much too fond of horses to make much of a success in the ranching business. She insisted I pay the taxes on our land, too, but it turned out that Rusty's lawyer was there ahead of us. It sometimes troubles me to be wed to a girl who is older, smarter and better-mannered than I am, but I work hard, and burn the midnight oil trying to improve myself, having matriculated in the English Grammar term at Prof. Plough's Latin College—the results of which study I ask you, dear reader, to be judge.